I0542049

SEASONED WOMEN
Volume Two

Winter's Thaw

Spring Training

STACEY LYNN RHODES

Seasoned Women Volume Two
ISBN # 978-1-78430-081-4
©Copyright Stacey Lynn Rhodes 2014
Cover Art by Posh Gosh ©Copyright 2014
Interior text design by Claire Siemaszkiewicz
Totally Bound Publishing

Published in 2014 by Totally Bound Publishing, Newland House, The Point, Weaver Road, Lincoln, LN6 3QN, United Kingdom.

Totally Bound Publishing is an imprint of Total-E-Ntwined Limited.

WINTER'S THAW

Dedication

For Rebecca — thank you for all you do.

Chapter One

God, I hate Muzak. Maggie switched her cell phone to the other ear and pushed her fingers through her dark, irritatingly frizzed-out hair, automatically loosening yet another snag. She normally straightened and smoothed the mop, preferring it sleek, but hadn't had time this morning, so it fell in kinky twists, closely framing her cheeks.

It would probably be better covering her face entirely. She knew she looked like crap right now, between the lack of sleep and no makeup. She had just spent most of yesterday flying halfway across the country with her nine-year-old daughter, Cassie, to her mom's farm for an extended summer visit. Normally once they were there, they'd stay in and not see the light of day for a while until they started to go stir-crazy.

Then after dinner, just as they were settling in to watch a movie, the call had come about her husband, Wade…

Well, technically he was her *ex*-husband, but one month of 'ex' versus almost fifteen years of marriage made it hard to automatically add the prefix.

It had been the Highway Patrol with the shocking news that Wade had been transported to St Vincent's after a multiple-car accident. They hadn't given her any other details, instructing her to call the hospital for more information. She'd immediately left the room to keep from alerting Cassie to the problem and got on the phone to St Vincent's. She'd been redirected a couple of times from the switchboard to the Emergency Room then had finally gotten through to someone who could answer her questions. Once they'd confirmed her identity, she'd learned Wade had been admitted and was in critical condition in the ICU. He'd been unconscious since his arrival.

Stunned and worried, she'd booked a flight for first thing the next morning, deciding to leave Cassie with Mom instead of dragging her right back home. Maggie had then spent a mostly sleepless night getting frequent updates from the nurses before driving alone in the bleak pre-dawn to the closest airport. It was a bit surreal to be back in the same place she'd just been through less than a day prior.

The first short commuter flight to the bigger regional hub had gone fine, and a voicemail message to call the ICU had been waiting when she turned her cell phone back on after disembarking.

She continued to wait on hold, listening to the light jazz music, and glanced up automatically as an extremely tall man stepped over her stretched-out legs before dropping into the seat next to her. Mouth going dry, she could only just keep from gawking.

You don't see a guy like that every day. Wow, talk about the total package.

She made a mental note to tell her best friend, Sam, that she had sat right next to a Total Stud. Maybe even a Fallen Angel, their highest ranking for hot über-alpha male.

She gave him a quick, furtive once-over out of the corner of her eye, her clearest view of his body his lap, where jeans that looked older than him lovingly clung.

Holy smokes. And 'package' was certainly right on the money.

He might have gone with comfort on the lower half, but had dressed it up with a button-down shirt and sports coat, and the combination definitely worked on him.

More than just an Angel. They might have to invent a whole new category just for him, she mused. Maybe 'God on Earth?' She searched her imagination for a title worthy of him as she continued to hold. The two friends had played this game for years, 'collecting' and describing in detail the yummy, unattainable eye-candy they ran across. They were married, they always joked, not blind. Though, Maggie had to remind herself once again, she was single now, not that it made much difference. Scenery was all it was. Guys like that never looked twice at middle-aged moms.

At least she had something to keep her mind occupied while she was stuck in phone purgatory.

* * * *

"I'm sorry," the older woman's impersonal voice rang through the brutally clear cell connection. This was breaking it to her gently? "Someone from the discharge planning office will be calling about making arrangements and getting your husband's effects back to you." The delivery was rote, as if she was reading from a mental script. "Mrs Winter?" she prodded.

"Yes, fine," Maggie managed to croak out. "Thank you." *What am I thanking her for? For telling me that my husband just died? Talk about a social oddity.* The call disconnected, apparently from the other end, and Maggie was left leaning back in the hard airport seat, cupping her cell phone loosely in a slightly trembling hand.

The white noise from the endless mass of humanity around her was a surreal backdrop to the chaos in her mind. Maggie sat there motionless for an untold measure of time, until a sudden, energetic surge of movement around her brought her back to the current situation. Apparently, they were boarding.

Stay or go? The call had been an abrupt ending to a flurry of planning and rushing about which had started about fifteen hours earlier when she had gotten that first unexpected call from the Highway Patrol.

Now, she was sitting here in the Minneapolis airport, standby the best she could do for this upcoming flight, and suddenly, she wasn't even sure if she should continue to Oregon or return to her daughter.

Cass.

A fresh burst of pain hit and Maggie sighed wearily at the prospect of breaking the news to her daughter. She rubbed her forehead, feeling the tension headache that had been growing all day tighten, digging its claws in. Poor baby was going to be devastated. Regardless of the difficulties Wade and Maggie had gone through lately as a couple, Cassie was very attached to her dad. Maggie flashed on a recent memory of Wade, energetic and in the prime of life, hoisting Cassie up in the air and mock-complaining about how big she was getting. Then tried to picture him lying on a hospital bed, still, unmoving, not breathing…

Maggie teared up and blinked, firmly pushing the impossible image away, swallowing hard as she debated her next move. The prospect of flying home alone and walking into the house they'd once shared was just disturbing. She should probably just go to customer service and catch the next available short flight back to her mom and daughter.

Her name being forcefully announced penetrated her mental anguish. "That's passengers Ingram, party of two, and Winter, for Portland. Please come to the podium," the gate attendant repeated over the intercom, and Maggie stood to automatically obey. Taking a step to the right, she collided with something immoveable and began to wobble. Before gravity took over, a firm grip caught her elbow and steadied her. She looked gratefully down into a pair of intense blue eyes. *Ah yes, the God on Earth.*

"Thanks." Maggie shook her head, feeling disconnected to reality. "Sorry about that."

"No problem," Blue-Eyes returned sympathetically. "Least I could do. My bag, my bad." He continued to hold her arm in a gentle grip. Maggie raised an eyebrow, and he released her with a faint, apologetic smile that had her smiling slightly in return.

She sobered abruptly with a mental slap that felt almost like a physical blow. *Your husband is dead, Mags, nothing to smile about right now.* She wondered numbly how many hundreds of times the reality would brutally hit her like that before she remembered.

Maggie shouldered the mom-sized leather purse which was her only bag for the trip, a deliberate attempt to avoid having to battle for overhead storage. She worked her way through the maze of legs and bags to the counter, waiting behind an older couple with matching wheeled luggage who had gotten there just ahead of her.

"Hi," the male gate attendant greeted the couple. "Ingram?" The pair nodded in sync, the frowning wife bellying up to the counter. "There's one seat in first class that I can put you in, and the other is in coach."

"Aren't there two seats together?"

Maggie mentally rolled her eyes at the woman's pointless question. The harried attendant looked irritated. "Well, there are two seats in coach, however, they aren't right next to each other. Middle seats"—he glanced down at the screen—"only two rows away from each other. I assumed one of you would prefer the first-class seat."

"But we're traveling *together*. There must be something you can do." She leaned aggressively across the counter. Mr Ingram stood back, apparently accustomed to letting his wife duke it out on their behalf. "I'm not going to sit between two strangers for four hours. Aren't there two first-class seats?"

This time, Maggie did roll her eyes, and let out an audible sigh that felt really good. *Yes, just for you, lady, we'll put an extra row in the plane.* Her head was really starting to pound.

"Honey," Mr Ingram timidly chimed in. "Why don't you take the first-class seat? I don't mind."

"Well, I do!" She rounded on him. "This is ridiculous. Just because you didn't make sure we had seat assignments when you reserved this trip..." She turned her ire on her husband, and Maggie tried to tune them out, though it was hard at this close range.

The airline employee looked past them to Maggie. "Winter?" he queried, and she nodded. He typed for a few seconds without further comment, then the sound of printing came from under the counter. He reached down and extracted a boarding pass, which he stretched over the counter to pass to Maggie. So simple. She glanced down. Seat two-F.

"Thank you." She offered the gate attendant her first genuine smile of the day.

And there you have it. Flies, honey, vinegar. Point proven.

He smiled back and gave her a conspiratorial wink. Maggie strode to the dwindling line to board. She wanted to make sure to get into her seat before the arguing couple realized that the first-class seat was history.

With that distraction gone, she began thinking again about Wade. They'd had a solid marriage up until the past year when things had crumbled. But even during the amicable divorce, which had become final last month, for the most part they'd been able to keep things happy and friendly for Cassie's sake. After well over two decades together, he was still a huge part of Maggie's life. Yet she felt completely numb. *Shouldn't I be crying or something?*

Maggie remembered bursting into tears immediately when she'd learned her own dad had died. She'd literally cried for days. Still did sometimes, five years later. But in the unexpected face of her loss today, her eyes remained dry.

She clenched her jaw, miserable and furious with herself. *What the hell's wrong with me? And why am I even going to Portland now?* She stopped abruptly on her way down the gangway as that thought penetrated. She had forgotten all about deciding she should probably just go back to Mom's. The sole reason she had been going home was to be with Wade while he was in the hospital. Now…

Maggie groaned. The overwhelming scope of all she suddenly had to do in the next few days began to whirl through her aching head. She pushed it aside and tried to focus on this trip. Might as well go home at this point, she decided wearily. Surely some of the details would be easier to handle there in person rather than over the phone. She finished her descent down the gangway, stepping onto the plane without acknowledging the cheerful generic greeting of the flight attendant. *Two-F*, she recalled, looking to the left at the numbers along the overhead bins then looking down…to meet the now-familiar blue eyes belonging to the man in the aisle seat next to hers.

Blue-Eyes had evidently been watching her approach—she'd caught him in the process of rising from his seat. Her eyes followed him up, her head tilting slightly upward as he continued to rise well past six feet. He'd lost the jacket somewhere along the way, so this time she got a perfect view of his wide, developed chest, well-displayed by his fitted white shirt tucked into those impossibly faded jeans. She forced herself to look away, mentally chiding herself as he stepped into the aisle.

Geez, quit panting like an idiot over this hard, young kid, Maggie Jean. Drooling is very unbecoming at your age. And hardly the time or the place for it.

He made a gentlemanly gesture toward the window seat, and she slid past him, only a breath away from that wall of chest, before twisting to sit heavily. As he settled in next to her, she automatically bent to tuck her purse under the seat. After sitting back up, Maggie slumped as she realized she needed to, at the very least, tell her mom the news. She bent again with a sigh, rummaging for her cell phone.

Blue-Eyes was quiet beside her. There was nothing to keep her from making this call. Nothing except the fact that it would make all of this real.

With another, heavier sigh, she speed-dialed her mom.

"Hello?" The breathy greeting came just when Maggie was sure it would go over to voicemail and she wondered what Cass had roped Grandma into doing.

"Hey, Mom," she responded. "How's everything going with Cass?"

"We're just fine, honey. Finished breakfast a little while ago and we're playing Scrabble out in the sunroom. Have you heard anything new?"

Maggie took a deep breath, nostrils flaring. She couldn't believe she had to say this. "He died, Mom."

"What? Oh, Mags…"

She closed her eyes as her mom's shocked exclamation was mostly lost under the announcement from the flight attendant telling everyone to stow their electronic devices. "I've got to go," she managed to get out through her tight throat. "I'm on the plane to Portland and they're closing up. And Mom?" she added quickly. "Please don't tell Cass yet, okay? I'll talk to her when I get back in a few days. I…want to do it in person."

"Oh my God, honey, I'm so, so sorry. Call me as soon as you get home."

"Okay, will do. Bye, Mom." Maggie closed the phone, then popped it back open again as another detail occurred to her. *Home. Crap, I am so unprepared for all this.*

She dialed her friend. And this time she did get voicemail. *Damn.* "Hey Sam, it's me. Uh, I'm on my way back home. Long story I don't want to go into right now, but I was looking for a ride from the airport this afternoon. I'll just go ahead and grab a taxi or something. I'll call you later, okay?" She disconnected then turned her phone off and tucked it back into her bag. Now without any connection to the outside world, she would have around four hours of quiet during the flight before she arrived home and had to dive into this mess. Maggie heaved a deep sigh, sagging bonelessly back against the seat. She closed her eyes for a few seconds before the flight attendant made a loud announcement about passengers needing to finish stowing their luggage and take their seats.

When she dragged them back open, she blinked in surprise. She'd nearly forgotten about her seatmate.

Now on rotation for her viewing pleasure were Blue-Eyes' long legs, stretched out under the seat in front of him and crossed at the ankles. His large, strong hand rested on the armrest between them, long fingers drumming occasionally. He was tan, as though he either worked outdoors or had just spent a lot of time in the sun. For some reason, the way his forearm and hand moved as he fidgeted sent a spike of feeling shooting through her gut.

"Would you like something to drink?" This question was from the flight attendant, as she set a napkin on the area between the armrests, her manicured hand lingering close to Blue-Eyes' forearm. Unwarranted irritation made Maggie's mouth tighten as she looked up and found the flight attendant practically in Blue-Eyes' lap as she bent over him. It had to be against airline regulations to have her shirt unbuttoned that far down.

To Maggie's shock, Blue-Eyes picked up her own hand, his fingers toying with her diamond engagement ring. She still wore it, even though she no longer kept on her wedding band. After so long, her ring finger felt naked without something on it. She supposed at some point she'd put this one away, too.

He leaned closer to her. "Do you want something?"

Her gaze snapped to his, uncomprehending, as her jaw dropped in shock. There was a teasing glint, but also a bit of sympathy there. *What is he doing?* The strokes of his fingers on hers were doing something wicked to her insides.

"Let's start with some water. She has a bad headache." This was directed to the flight attendant. "Do you have anything she can take for the pain?"

Maggie watched as the attendant withdrew to the galley, then turned back to Blue-Eyes. "She's gone now. You can let go," she whispered hoarsely, trying in vain to reclaim her hand.

"But she'll be back," he murmured. He bent his head toward hers again. His dark hair looked like it had been recently cut in a short, businesslike style with a slight wave, and his chiseled jaw line sported a hint of shadow. His fingers stopped moving, but he continued to hold her hand. Maggie could feel the warmth spreading upwards from her chest to her face as the blush consumed her. How long had it been since she'd sat holding hands like a kid on a date? Wade wasn't one for PDA. That thought did the sudden smack of reality thing again, which only added to her anxiety.

She turned away to try to get herself under control and could hear Blue-Eyes thanking the flight attendant. She gave a surreptitious tug to her left hand, practically a yank. He refused to relinquish it immediately but gently turned her hand over and placed a small pack containing two pills in her palm.

"Are these okay?" he asked, indicating the medicine in her hand. She glanced down and nodded. He held a glass of water, which he gestured with. "Go ahead."

She ripped open the package and tipped the pills onto her tongue then reached for the glass. Her fingers brushed his as she took it, and she mentally castigated herself as she swallowed the water. *C'mon, Mags. Hardly a good time to get caught up flirting with some airplane Romeo.*

That thought sobered her again, and she knew she had to nip this in the bud as she finished the glass of water and set it down. "Thank you," she offered blandly, without looking at him.

The heat his attention had set off inside her became overwhelming in combination with the stagnant air of the plane. The circulation didn't seem to be going—maybe because they were preparing for takeoff. But she needed to cool down, so she shrugged out of the light linen jacket she'd worn, even though summer was in full force, in order to help combat the unpredictable cabin temperatures that could see-saw during flight. She thought about flagging down the over-styled attendant and having her hang it up, but then she'd have to deal with her if she got cold later. She rolled it up loosely and tucked it in the gap between her purse handles. Feeling Blue-Eyes watching her, she pointedly closed her eyes and leaned back.

She continued to sense his regard, but stubbornly refused to acknowledge him and tried to relax. It felt so good to close her eyes. This was her fourth flight in two days.

Her eyes flew open in shock and she gasped as she felt a butterfly-light, glancing touch across her left breast. Her nipples instantly hardened to taut peaks, and she saw Blue-Eyes' arm as he reached across her chest.

"Sorry. Seatbelt," he explained as he located the end on the window side, which she had been sitting on. She shifted as he tugged it out from under her ass then buckled her in. "You forgot to fasten it. I thought you were almost asleep. I was really trying not to bother you. Seems like you need the rest." He gave her one last look, an empathetic one. Of course, he'd overheard her telling Mom about Wade dying. Even if he didn't know who she'd been talking about, he recognized how it affected her. He'd been nothing but understanding and chivalrous so far, so likely he was telling the truth about not wanting to bother her and not just trying to cop a feel.

That reminded her of her body's instant reaction to his touch and she inhaled, trying not to look at her chest to see just how prominent her nipples were against her blouse. His eyelashes swept downwards and she could feel the tension seem to ratchet up about ten notches.

She met his eyes again and the empathy had shifted to include a touch of heated appreciation. Maggie squirmed a little under his gaze. Had she ever been on the receiving end of a look like that from a guy like him? Never in her very ordinary life. She closed her eyes again, a little desperately, resisting the almost overwhelming urge to cross her arms across her chest. Apparently, Blue-Eyes finally got the message, since he also settled back into his seat.

Gradually she relaxed, and the plane taxied, made the turn then accelerated toward takeoff. She was hyperaware of her body and could feel her breasts jouncing slightly as the plane moved over the runway. Was he watching? Just the thought made her nipples peak again. A slight movement next to her made her wish for a blanket.

She had thrown together an outfit that morning by grabbing the first few things she pulled out of her suitcase that went together. The bra she had on was a comfortable one of red nylon—pretty and lacy and light, but not exactly the most supportive. Now she wished she had some armor to rein in her wayward breasts, even if it would have been uncomfortable to wear. Her nipples seemed to be eagerly awaiting the next touch.

Party's over, ladies.

Chapter Two

Nick rested back against the seat, shifting slightly. What was it about this petite woman that made him feel protective and aroused all at once? He had noticed her in the waiting area for the flight and purposely taken the seat next to her. For all the good that had done. He had immediately spied the disappointing presence of her wedding band. *Figures. Of course someone like her is married.* She had barely even noticed him before he caught her as she tripped on his bag.

He had still been thrilled when he'd realized that she was his seatmate for the flight, not that he expected anything more than some conversation. He wasn't the type to poach, but she looked like she was having a hard time of it, which had also sparked the caregiving side of him. With their proximity, he had had no choice but to eavesdrop on her phone calls, watching in empathy as she had passed along the bad news to her mother. He wasn't sure who had died, but suspected it was her husband. He felt like the biggest asshole in the world for his earlier resentment of her married state.

Jesus, you're a creep.

He should have just left her alone, but there was that air of fragility about her that made him want to ease whatever stress he could from her. Nick wasn't sure what had possessed him to seize the flimsy excuse provided by the hovering flight attendant to take her hand, except for maybe wishful thinking and the hope that she needed some human contact. She looked so lost. But once he touched her, he just couldn't stop.

Her hand was so soft and warm, so small in his. He had tugged at her ring. It didn't look like a wedding band, more like an engagement ring, but what did he know? The wave of possessiveness that went through him as he toyed with it had stunned him. He'd never before felt strongly enough about any woman he'd dated to consider the type of commitment needed to require that sort of public display — to place a ring on his partner's finger for all to see. But as he'd played with the ring, he'd flashed to an imagining of how that might be.

Her eyes were a beautiful burnished copper as they'd widened in surprise at his touch, and he could see the pain and stress lurking in their depths. A headache, he'd guessed, and no wonder.

He had honestly been just trying to help her get settled when he reached across her to buckle her seatbelt. But the back of his arm had glanced across her breast, and he had felt the peak pressing back against his skin. He hadn't been able to resist a glance down. A slight glimpse of a lacy red bra had been visible where her blouse gaped between the buttons.

He groaned inwardly now at the recollection. He raked a hand through his hair and leaned back in his seat, careful not to touch her again. Her eyes were closed. However, he somehow knew she was as aware of him as he was of her.

Nick took the opportunity to surreptitiously study her profile as the plane began to take off. Her skin was fair with light freckles scattered across her tilted nose and cheekbones, and at this close range, just a few permanent smile lines were visible. No makeup. He guessed she was probably a bit older than him, likely in her thirties. Her almost-curly, dark hair was past shoulder-length with some lighter glints to it. With those pretty amber eyes instead of the usual blue or ordinary brown, she made an impression. Her hands were clasped across her slim waist, and like him, she wore jeans, which hugged her generous hips and fell to straight legs. She had comfortable-looking sport sandals on, and her legs were stretched out in front of her, loosely crossed at the ankles.

Nick let his gaze drift back up her still form to her simple red blouse. As if she felt his regard, her nipples hardened again, poking at the soft fabric. He sucked in a breath in reaction as he shifted once more. She was blushing again, but her eyes were screwed closed and he reluctantly looked away, trying to respect her obvious desire for privacy.

As the plane began to level off, sensing she was still awake, he finally lost patience, wanting to see her eyes again.

"I'm Nick."

She continued to rest her head on the seatback, but tilted his way as those heart-stopping eyes opened to zero in on his. The effect was somehow very private and personal, as if he was her sole focus. "Maggie." She blinked and averted her gaze to somewhere in the vicinity of his shoulder. "I'm sorry if I'm being rude, but I've had a really bad day, and I just need to get some rest."

Even as she voiced her desire for privacy, she angled slightly toward him.

"So I gathered. I'm sorry—I couldn't help but overhear your phone conversations." Emboldened by her body language, he took her hand again. "You lost someone today?" he queried in a soft tone of voice.

Maggie felt the first prick of tears in response to his unsolicited sympathy. "My...husband, Wade," she managed. *Oh no.* She could feel the tears building as she spoke his name out loud for the first time since she'd gotten the news.

Finally beginning to grasp her loss, feeling the dam breaking, she tried to avoid embarrassment and turned away toward the window. Nick took her by the shoulders and pulled her back firmly against his chest, leaning awkwardly across the center console between them, silently holding her as she at last began to weep.

After a couple of minutes of the grief overwhelming her, reality began to intrude. The position wasn't in the least comfortable with the hard plastic pressing into her lower back, and as if sensing this, Nick leaned forward, easing her more upright as she struggled to get a handle on her emotions, though he kept her braced against him.

As if breaking down and sobbing in the arms of a complete stranger wasn't bad enough, the flight attendant chose then to come back around and refill drink orders. She reached their row and waited, somewhat impatiently, for their attention.

"Nothing right now." Nick's voice came from right by Maggie's ear as the corresponding rumble in his chest gave her the awareness she needed to pull away. He slowly let her go, allowing her to straighten, and she immediately dove for her purse, needing a tissue in the worst way. She appreciated the gestures, both comforting her then giving her some space, but she missed the support of his strong embrace now that it was gone.

Throat aching and a million thoughts racing through her head, she settled back once again in her seat and stared blankly out of the window at the blue sky and wondered at the surreal scene she'd somehow fallen into. Back and forth across the country. Falling into the sympathetic arms of a disarmingly gorgeous man.

Oh, and losing Wade.

Forever.

Maggie shook her head as if that could clear her mind. She couldn't remember a time when he hadn't been in her life. She and Wade had been high school sweethearts — well, junior high to tell the truth. They'd gone on to the same college together, been each other's best friend, married soon after graduation and eventually had Cassie. Everything should have been rosy.

The only portion of their lives that hadn't really clicked was what had eventually driven them apart. Sex. Or lack thereof. Wade had a high sex drive, while Maggie's was nearly non-existent, even more so since she'd had Cass. He had begun to resent always being the initiator and she in turn had felt pressured and harassed. Finally, perhaps inevitably, Wade had strayed outside their marriage. His affair had been brief, and many men would likely have hidden the secret relationship away, but in this their long friendship had stood them in good stead. So they'd talked about it as rationally as they could, and the separation had come with pangs of nostalgia, but no real pain.

The divorce had been, according to her friend Sam, 'ridiculously amicable,' and they were even technically still sharing the house. Wade had an apartment a couple of miles away. But instead of having Cassie uproot herself for his portion of the visitation, Wade just kept a bedroom in their house and stayed over most weekends, as if the family unit was still whole. They'd agreed that when—or, as she'd always silently amended in her case, *if*—they ever started seeing other people, that would be time enough to begin to completely disentangle their lives. But for now, it worked for them.

Had worked.

The bludgeoning mental correction to past tense shook Maggie to the core once again. Her thoughts opened her eyes to the realization that she'd be home in a few hours, walking into the house they'd shared—alone. She could probably go stay at Sam's, but that was ridiculous. It was her home.

Nick had been a quiet presence next to her while she'd composed herself, and she was grateful for his understanding. Pushing all thoughts aside for now, Maggie accepted the warm towel to wash up before the meal arrived. She'd had a somewhat confused moment when the flight attendant had held it out to her with tongs, but had followed Nick's lead in using it to wash her hands. *Do they always do this in first class? Who knew?* No wonder they pulled the curtain between them and the rest of the plane. Maggie smiled slightly as she wondered what the flight attendant's reaction would have been if she'd taken it and used it to wipe down her face or maybe drape it across her neck for the warm heat to relieve the tension there. Come to think of it, she really could use a trip to the lav to splash some cold water on her face. The tear tracks had dried and felt a bit crusty and tight and God knew how bad her eyes looked at the moment. Thankfully, she hadn't worn makeup today. But they were probably red and puffy. She had some eye drops in her purse, she remembered.

Maggie stood and Nick followed suit in order to let her out. She was struck again by his height next to hers. Wade had only been four or five inches taller than her, so the way Nick loomed over her as she passed him and he looked down at her with concern sent a visceral flutter through her chest at his proximity.

Once she'd retreated behind the door of the lav, she grimaced at herself in the mirror. Even taking into account the unflattering light, it wasn't a pretty sight. She wasn't trying to impress anyone, but she had her pride. Maggie freshened up, taking time to splash her face with cool water, then made good use of her eye drops and some lotion since her skin was already starting to feel dry.

The meal service had already begun when she emerged and dodged the busy attendant. It looked as though their row had been skipped, which didn't really bother her any. She had no appetite at the moment.

Nick rose in order to let her in. "I asked her to wait to serve us after you came back. There's more than one choice of entrée and I wasn't sure what would appeal to you." His eyes took her in and he gave her a reassuring smile.

Touched, she reflected that someone had definitely been looking out for her in the seatmate department.

She took her seat. "Thank you. But you didn't have to wait for me."

"It's okay. Better to not have to move my things. And I was raised better than that. My mom would have given me 'the look' if she knew I started eating before a lady."

That coaxed a smile from her. "Old-fashioned mom?"

Nick narrowed his eyes thoughtfully. "Not particularly in her ideas on things, but she was from the East Coast and her family was well-off. Old money. They entertained a lot, and so social manners were a big thing with them." He grinned. "She made sure we knew which utensil to use so we wouldn't embarrass her when we went back to Grandmother's. But she's pretty liberal in her thinking and can do the secret eye-roll with the best of them when the stuffed shirts get going on certain topics. Like this…"

The flight attendant had returned to take their choices for their entrées and he had her smiling as he demonstrated the surreptitious eye-roll. Nick's humorous account of his mom's antics continued until the food came.

After a murmured *"Bon appétit"* from Nick, they shared their meal in a not uncomfortable silence. He really was a good companion. He seemed to know exactly when to talk and when to give her space.

Maggie struggled to find any enjoyment in the surprisingly good food, but knew she had to get something into her stomach. She slowly ate as much as she could, trying to focus on each bite. After things had been cleared away and they'd stowed their tables back in the armrests, Maggie found herself turning to the man next to her.

She opened her mouth to speak, then found she didn't know quite what to say and closed it again, but his attention had already been garnered. *Oh well.* She was struggling for a grip on some sort of conversational ball when he thankfully jumped in instead.

"Would you like something else to drink?"

Maggie was stuffed and the thought of adding more was unappealing. "No, but thanks for asking." She took a deep breath then exhaled. Part of her wanted to talk but her mind was so scattered at the moment she just couldn't seem to settle on any kind of direction to take a conversation.

The silence stretched on as he waited expectantly.

What's wrong with me? This guy has me tongue-tied.

She wasn't sure she liked the implications of that realization. She usually wasn't one to be concerned about the expectations of others though for some reason she didn't want Nick to have a poor opinion of her.

Chapter Three

Nick waited for Maggie to say something, but took mercy on her when she seemed stymied for a topic. "How is your head feeling?"

She blinked and took a moment before she answered, "It's okay. Better, but still just...full."

He could only imagine. "You want to talk about it, or do idle chit-chat?"

She sent a grateful look his way. "Chit-chat is good."

So they spent the next half hour talking about random things, and if periodically she would steer away from certain topics, likely linked in her mind to the elephant in the room, he let her direct the flow.

The video compilation finally settled into the movie, and they donned their headphones. Nick really had no interest in watching the rom-com, but went ahead for appearances' sake to take some of the pressure off Maggie — that strange compulsion to talk to the person next to you on a flight. He felt sort of bad for talking her ear off for the last while, but she'd demonstrated earlier that she had no qualms about tuning people out when she really wanted to, so he could only assume that their rambling conversation was serving as a distraction of sorts from her current situation. He'd been through enough training on grief before in his line of work to know that people reacted in different ways but needing the appearance of normalcy was very common.

When the movie finished, they'd been sitting next to one another for hours, and Nick reflected that the sheer proximity gave him a sort of comfortable knowledge of Maggie. Oh, she still pushed his buttons, but he was in his twenties, not some out-of-control hormonal kid. So the low-level glow of attraction simply warmed, an undertone to the ease with which he was becoming familiar with his seatmate.

The delicate way she picked at her food first before visibly forcing herself to eat. The constant shifting in her seat, which spoke of being unused to sitting for such a long stretch. Her clothing choices, which put comfort ahead of trends. All these observations combined to paint a picture of her in Nick's mind — one of a woman who concentrated less on herself and more on the people and activities around her. She was well-spoken and polite, even with the trauma she was currently undergoing, and she most definitely loved her dead husband.

Nick shook his head in sad wonder. To have such a deep connection then lose it so suddenly... It was amazing she was doing as well as she was. She was probably still in shock, he decided, and he hoped she had someone in town to support her when she got back. That brought his mind back around to the message he'd heard her leave earlier.

Touching her soft hand briefly to get her attention startled her into focusing on him, then she offered him a half-smile that looked at home on her face. He smiled in return. Obviously asking her how she was would be the dumbest question ever, so he amended it to, "Still feeling okay? Sorry, you were kind of lost in thought. But it just occurred to me that I wanted to make sure you had a ride home from the airport."

A slight grimace crossed her face. "I won't know until I land, I guess. I wasn't able to get hold of Sam — my friend," she clarified and he nodded. "I'll probably just take a taxi. It's the weekend, so the light rail doesn't run out to my neck of the woods."

"You live down in the southwest 'burbs? That's a long taxi ride."

She shrugged. "Works both ways. By the time I get hold of Sam then wait for her to get to the airport, I could be home already, even by taxi."

He made the offer that had been circling in his head. "My car's in the airport parking garage, and I live down that way. I don't mind giving you a ride."

Her gaze turned wary, and he figured she was thinking about getting into a car with a virtual stranger, having him know where she lived. He held up a hand. "Only if you're comfortable with that. But honestly, I live in Lake Grove, so I have to go down there anyway, and I can guarantee my car's more comfortable than a taxi." He smiled reassuringly then had an idea. He pulled out his wallet and extracted his license.

"Here." He handed it to her. "You can text my info to whoever you like when we land so someone knows who you're with, if that makes you feel safer." He watched as she studied his ID for a minute, then looked up at him, startled.

She scrutinized him. "You're younger than you look."

Nick burst out laughing. "Should I feel insulted that I look 'old'?" he teased, and watched as a blush crept up her neck and face.

"I didn't say that...exactly. Just old-*er*. Than you actually are. Oh, man." She dropped her face into her hands and groaned theatrically, and Nick felt a burst of affection for her. At least he'd gotten her mind off things for a moment.

"It's okay. See? I'm of legal age and everything."

"Barely," she mumbled under her breath, but he managed to catch it even under the white noise of the plane.

"Oh, come on. You're not that much older than I am."

She finally peeked back over at him, this time with her brow arched skeptically. "Well, you just keep on thinking that. That's fine with me. As for me, I *know* exactly how much older I am, so I'm entitled to comment."

She maintained her serious look for a few moments then they were both laughing. She handed his ID back and caught his hand for a moment. The grip surprised him and sent a shiver of awareness through him.

"In all seriousness, thank you." She gestured around them. "For everything. I was really dreading this flight. I don't do well with a lot of time to think, and... Well, you've made it pass by much more easily than I ever would have guessed possible." She glanced at their joined hands and let go quickly. "And thanks also for the offer of a ride, but I don't want to put you out."

"It's no trouble at all," Nick interjected, sensing that she was wavering. He put all his sincerity into the gaze he locked with hers. "I'm happy to do it, if it will make this day any less stressful for you."

Maggie's cheeks puffed out as she blew out a quick breath. "I never do this, have anything to do with strangers…"

"We're not really strangers anymore, are we?" Nick heard the overly serious tone of his own voice and purposely lightened it up. "I mean, you cried all over me, we've held hands, heck, even the flight attendant thinks we're together."

He got his desired response as her lips turned up in a slight smile once again. "Okay, that would be really nice. I'm not a huge fan of taxis." Her nose wrinkled up.

How adorable is that?

A shadow crossed her face as her expression smoothed out once again.

"What is it?" he gently queried.

She shrugged then hugged herself. "I was just thinking about walking into the house. Alone. It's never empty. I mean…" She looked out of the window pensively. "Between me and Wade and Cass and Champ — the cat, who's with Sam," she explained and he nodded. "It's…just going to seem really quiet."

He didn't have a response for that, so kept silent, letting her follow her own thoughts. After a moment, she shook herself out of her ponderings and shot him a curious glance. "You're awfully comfortable with this. Are you some kind of counselor or something?"

"Or something," he agreed. "I'm a police officer."

Her eyebrows rose. "Really?" she blurted, then grimaced apologetically. "I don't know why that surprises me, but it does." She looked puzzled. "You might have mentioned that when you were trying to get me to trust you enough to take a ride from you."

Nick frowned, hoping she wasn't that naïve. "You wouldn't trust someone just because they *said* they were in law enforcement, would you?" She appeared to think for a moment then shook her head decisively. He relaxed a bit. "Good." He reached in his other back pocket and pulled out his flat badge and departmental ID in their slim case and opened it for her to see. "Always ask to see their ID. Most departments require we carry our credentials at all times while armed, which is most of the time. Oh, not right now," he clarified as her eyebrows shot upwards and her eyes dropped to scan his waistline. He tucked his ID back away. "But I'm just in the habit of having it on me."

"Okay," she acknowledged, and he wondered what was going on behind those wary eyes. "I guess I am a bit naïve." She had somehow plucked the word right out of his head. "I don't know much about cops... Uh, is 'cops' okay?"

He nodded, amused at her worried expression. "I've been called worse," he commented wryly.

Her lips twitched and he had to look away from her as some very inappropriate thoughts went through his head. He looked at his wristwatch. One more hour.

Nick shifted uncomfortably as her scent and nearness and the intimacy of their more relaxed conversation combined to make his cock start to thicken. *Damn it.* He finally gave up and headed to the lav for a little breathing room before he shocked her with an inappropriate display.

He washed up but didn't linger in the small space. Just meeting his own somber eyes in the mirror had been enough to quell his out-of-the-blue reaction. Maggie was dealing with a life-changing tragedy right now, and he needed to concentrate on doing what he could to help make things easier for her.

When he walked out of the door, his eyes went straight to Maggie, who was watching him come out.

It sent a smile of greeting to his lips. She followed him with her gaze as he walked toward her, and he couldn't help but feel a bit of pleasure that she had perhaps missed him while he'd been gone.

"Hi. Miss me?" he teased, wanting to see her smile again.

He was rewarded with a pursing of her lips as she tried not to react to his humor. "Oh, did you go somewhere?" she joked back.

He couldn't stop the grin that spread across his face. It was nice to see her spirits lighten a bit. He knew in a very short time she would be plunged into a very emotional and stressful situation. "Just ran to the store and the gym."

Maggie's eyebrows shot up. "Wait, I thought you were going to the dry cleaners."

That surprised a laugh out of him. She was quick. "They were closed, so I didn't want to waste a trip out. I mean, it's a looong way to go for no reason." He glanced pointedly out of the window and down toward the earth.

She giggled and the sound seemed to trigger some sort of realization in her, because she immediately sobered. He instantly missed her smile.

"Hey. It's okay to have a laugh or two," he tried to reassure her. "There's nothing wrong or disrespectful about taking a break for a short time. It does your body and mind good to have some relief from it." He patted her arm then withdrew his touch. "Try to remember that in the days and weeks to come. Okay?"

Her uncertain gaze was glued to his. "Wow. How did you know what I was thinking? About it not being appropriate to laugh under the circumstances, or even just"—she waved her hand around—"take a mental break from the reality of it, as you said. Must come from being a police officer."

Nick didn't want to say that he felt particularly in tune with her, more so than with people in general, so he took the easy route and just nodded his agreement. "That and you wear your emotions on your face. I could see the guilt after you caught yourself laughing, and you shouldn't feel guilty for being human."

Maggie cocked her head. "Huh. That's different. People usually tell me that I have a poker face. In fact, Wade used to say that—" She abruptly cut her words off.

"Wade used to say…" Nick prompted.

She had looked down at her hands in her lap. After a few moments, she turned to him again. "He used to say that he could never tell what I was thinking or feeling—that I was too stoic."

Nick frowned. He couldn't think of anyone less stoic than Maggie, though he had to acknowledge that he might be seeing a different side of her than most people in her life after so recently experiencing such a huge loss. "I don't see that at all," he finally responded with the truth.

"What do you see?" The question seemed to slip out before she had a chance to think about it.

Nick held her gaze as he turned more fully toward her. "I see a woman who feels things very deeply, who is utterly trustworthy and committed to the people she loves. I see someone who is struggling with how to cope with the unthinkable, yet is trying to put everyone else first. Most of all, I see a lovely human being, inside and out."

Her lips had parted during his heartfelt assessment and her cheeks had colored. Tears rose once again in her beautiful eyes.

"I'm sorry. Not for what I said," he clarified, "but because you have to go through this. And for making you cry again." He held out his arm and after a moment, she leaned against him across their barrier. They barely touched, just where her head came to rest on his upper chest and his arm across her shoulders, but those points radiated warmth straight to his heart.

It was just his luck that he'd finally run into a woman he felt true chemistry with, and she was a widow of less than a day. And right there, practically in his lap for hours.

Longest frickin' flight ever.

Chapter Four

"How do I ask this without sounding rude?" Maggie wondered aloud, not surprised when Nick tipped her a grin from the driver's seat of his SUV. He was a really likeable guy and she enjoyed their conversations. He was the kind of man she imagined people would gravitate to, take their troubles to and share things with they wouldn't tell other people. *Just look at me, I'm talking his ear off and making him play chauffeur for the 'damsel in distress'.*

"Lay it on me. If it's really rude, I'll just drop you off here." He waved his hand vaguely at the interstate highway rolling by under the vehicle.

She was unused to all this teasing and banter with a member of the opposite sex, but somehow he effortlessly brought it out of her. She found herself responding in kind. "Oh, that's too much. Police brutality!"

Nick's eyebrows shot up and for a moment, she thought she'd gone too far. Then a deep rumbling laugh built up and she spent the next couple of minutes trying not to smile as he regained his composure.

"You finished?" she mocked, checking her bare wrist for the elapsed time of his outburst of humor.

"Mmm-hmm." He was pressing his lips together. "You had a questionable question?"

She cleared her throat. "What were you doing flying first class?"

He huffed out a short laugh. "Oh, that *is* rude. What—you think because I'm a cop I should be stuck back in cattle class?"

Maggie sputtered for a minute before she noticed the teasing light in his eyes as he glanced away from the road at her. "Of course not," she answered, then conceded, "You got me. I thought you were seriously offended for a second there."

"Oh, I'm offended all right." He paused then clarified, "Offended that you don't think you can ask a reasonable question without me overreacting."

That's because I was married to the king of touchiness, she thought, then winced as she mentally chastised herself for thinking ill of the dead. "Touché."

Nick shrugged. "I'm a pretty big guy, I need the leg room. And I don't fly that often, but when I do, it's worth it to me to upgrade to first."

Her eyes had begun to roam over his form without conscious thought as he spoke, as if they needed to confirm he was indeed a big guy. Tall, yes—and muscular in a fit, athletic way. For the first time since she'd learned what he did for a living, Maggie tried to imagine him dressed for work, combining that physical strength with the authority of his uniform, and suddenly had an appreciation for how 'badge bunnies' must feel.

Okay, enough of that. Eyes forward.

Traffic wasn't too bad, and before long, Maggie was directing Nick to turn into her driveway. The house looked deserted in a way it never had before, even with the unforgiving daylight. He turned off the engine and Maggie still couldn't make herself move from the passenger's seat.

Then her door opened, and Nick stood there, a concerned expression on his face, holding his hand to her. Striving for courage, she swallowed and accepted his help, feeling the need for a connection, wanting to not feel alone right now.

"I'll walk you inside. Okay?"

Sheer relief made her a little dizzy. "Thank you."

She pulled out her keys and cell phone as they walked to the door. Maggie closed her eyes briefly at the thought of how many calls she was going to have to make, how many messages had piled up.

Maggie made herself stop thinking, unlock and open the front door. Despite her earlier thought of it feeling deserted, in actuality, the house looked no different than when she'd left it. *Why would it?* Maggie doubted Wade had been there in the brief time between their departure for the airport and his accident. In fact, ironically enough, that was exactly why Sam was watching Champ at her place instead of Wade checking on him here. Wade's apartment complex didn't allow pets and he had thought it would feel too quiet, too odd being here alone without Cass and Maggie.

Now here she was.

But not alone.

Nick stood in quiet support at her side in the foyer, looking around, his gaze sharp. *Ah, no wonder he wanted to walk me inside.* Probably hard to turn off the cop mentality, even when off duty.

She took another step farther inside and looked down as her foot contacted something. Cassie's Seattle Mariners hat. The one Wade had given her. She'd been wearing it when they were getting ready to leave for the airport, but had changed her mind and winged it in the door at the last minute. Maggie stooped to pick it up, memories of Cass and Wade interacting and smiling together in her head...and all at once, she broke down.

Nick tried to catch her arm as she pushed past him toward the couch, but she shook him off. Even in her sorrow, she knew she didn't want to make a fool of herself in front of him yet again. She willed him to leave as she dropped to the cushion, burying her face in her hands, but she wasn't terribly surprised when instead of going, Nick sat beside her and put a strong arm around her shoulders.

She must have wept for ages, and by the time the storm abated, she'd emptied the box of tissues on the end table and her shirt hem was soaked. Nick had retreated once and come back with a damp facecloth, which he used to cool her face. Maggie averted her eyes as she took it from him, and she hid behind the blessedly soothing material for as long as she could. It became evident he wasn't going anywhere anytime soon, and she finally gathered enough composure to surface from her roiling emotions.

"Don't you have anything better to do?" she challenged, her voice falling well short of the heat she'd intended.

"Not a thing," he replied with sincerity, and she raised her eyes to lock on him. He was so close to her. She was fully aware of what a disaster she must look, and very thankful she hadn't taken the time to put on any makeup when she'd touched up on the plane. At least she was spared the streaks down her face. But puffy and red likely wasn't much better. He'd definitely seen her at her worst since the time they'd met, and she felt an acute flare of embarrassment.

And yet she couldn't look away from him, trapped by the concern and warmth in his gaze.

"I'm a mess," she murmured, trying not to feel vain at the shallowness of her thoughts. Why did she care what he thought of her anyway?

"You're beautiful," he countered. "Just having a hard day. Totally understandable."

Her eyes dropped to his lips as he spoke and the sudden, random urge to kiss him both spooked and enticed her.

What are you thinking?

But her inner voice was more curious than chiding. She knew this was a bad idea. A really, really bad idea. But God help her, she wanted his touch right now, his strength, and she knew instinctively he wanted her too.

His lips were dry and warm against hers, gentle pressure as they glanced tentatively against one another. The contact shocked her into sanity and she pulled back with reluctance.

"Sorry about that," she apologized. For what, she wasn't certain.

"I'm not."

The husky answer sent a tendril of want coiling back through her, which she ruthlessly suppressed. Standing, she distanced herself from him, then fought back a yawn.

He stood as well. "You're tired. I should go."

"No." The automatic response surprised both of them. "I mean, of course you can go." She shook her head as if to clear it. "I can't think. I probably should have had you stop for a coffee."

"Would you like me to run and get you something?"

Just then, her forgotten cell phone rang. The sound immediately brought her back to the reality of all she needed to do. She answered the call from one of Wade's relatives and was quickly pulled into an emotional conversation. Nick stepped up to give her a brief hug and kiss on the forehead before mouthing, *"Hang in there. Okay?"* He turned and walked to the front door.

Her eyes followed him helplessly, and she wished she could say goodbye and thank him. The indefinable feeling she was losing something... That had to do with Wade. Right?

He lifted a hand in a wave then he was gone.

* * * *

The next couple of hours passed in an emotionally sapping blur of phone calls. Sam had come by to lend support for a time, but Maggie had soon sent her home with a promise to take her up on her offer of company tomorrow on numerous errands. She would need to go to the hospital to pick up Wade's things, the auto shop to address the car and probably Wade's apartment. And she would need to meet with the funeral director—not that they would be having a service right away. Wade had wanted to be cremated, so she gratefully decided to hold off on scheduling a memorial at least until after she'd told Cass. Wade's family was scattered across the country. Neither of his parents were alive, but he had several siblings and close cousins to consult with, most of whom had moved away from their hometown.

Every conversation had taken a little bit more out of her until the last one, which had sent her careening over the edge of vulnerable exhaustion—her goodnight phone call to Cass. She'd kept it as short as she could, Maggie's mom helping by successfully distracting Cass with the chance to choose dessert. The subterfuge of trying to act normal for her daughter's sake had sent Maggie crashing to the couch when the conversation ended, her mom's, "Try to get some rest, honey," echoing in her head as she finally succumbed to the welcome respite of sleep.

It was dark when she next stirred, something intruding into her uneasy rest. Then she was being lifted in strong arms and carried. The unfamiliar movement finally had her opening her eyes in dazed curiosity, even as she looped her arms around a masculine neck. Nick's scowl greeted her from a few inches away as he began to easily ascend the stairs, as though he weren't hauling a grown woman.

Maggie knew she should protest. She wondered at his presence in her house. But the past twenty-four hours had taken their toll and, still exhausted, she pushed all that aside and simply accepted the cosseting as Nick lowered her to her bed and covered her with an afghan.

"We're going to talk about you leaving the blinds open and the door unlocked." He grumbled his warning close to her ear then sighed. "But not now. Get some sleep." He straightened to go and the implications of his action finally cut through her lethargy.

She shot out a hand and grabbed his wrist before she knew what she'd planned. "Will you stay?" His shocked eyes met hers as he turned. "I mean...I didn't get a chance to say... I want to..." She let go of his wrist. "Oh, who am I kidding? I just…want you to stay." She inwardly pleaded for his understanding, because right then, she had no idea what she wanted or expected, whatever the outcome might be. Coherency was beyond her and if he asked her for a reason, she'd have no idea what to say.

All she knew was that when his arms had been around her, it was the only time she'd felt at peace all day. There was more to it than that, but that was all she'd allow herself at the moment.

His eyes searched hers in the dim light from the hallway then he stepped away from the bed once more. She bit back a protest—if he'd made up his mind to leave, there was no use in begging.

When he kicked off his shoes and placed them neatly under her dressing chair, she finally relaxed.

"I'm going to make sure everything's locked up and turn off the lights." He walked over and brushed some hair back from her temple. "Be right back."

Maggie exhaled in relief, then sat up as he strode from the room. It was one thing to fall asleep on the couch fully dressed, but if she was going to bed, she knew she'd rest better if she was comfortable. She made a trip to the bathroom, did an abbreviated night-time routine then slipped into one of her favorite old T-shirts. She briefly considered adding pajama pants, but knew she wouldn't be able to sleep as well, and the tee covered her almost to the knees anyway.

She was back in bed under the covers when Nick came back in. "Do you want me in here?" he asked, and didn't appear surprised when she took a deep breath and self-consciously nodded.

He walked to the opposite side of the bed and undid his jeans. That was when she noticed the gun. *Whoa.*

He must have noticed her eyes widening. "Does it bother you to have the gun in here? I usually keep it right next to me, but I can lock it in my —"

"No, that's fine. It just surprised me." She didn't really have a problem with it, but it had caught her off-guard.

He appeared to gauge her response then resumed, taking the holstered gun from his belt and placing it on the nightstand. Then he unselfconsciously dropped his pants.

Oh my God.

Maggie was instantly frustrated by the lack of light in the room. The tight white boxer briefs were like a beacon in the dark, but she couldn't see details.

Just as well, you perv. Go to sleep. Think of him as an asexual teddy bear.

Nick slipped his socks off and climbed into bed in his briefs and T-shirt. Maggie had a strange moment when the realization hit her that, yes, there was a man in her bed, and not one she'd known since they were kids. Wade had been her one and only since puberty, and they'd been friends for even longer. So to even be this close to another man was completely foreign, as were the sensations coursing through her. It took her a while to decipher what she felt and when she did, the shock of it almost killed the feeling itself.

Desire.

So this is what it feels like…

Stunned by the unfamiliar state, she instantly felt disloyal to her memory of Wade. If this was what had been missing from their relationship, if this was what she had owed him and never felt, then she had done him a great disservice in marrying him to begin with.

All those years, wasted.

Maggie curled onto her side, away from Nick, overwhelmed by her sorrow at finding out too late what should have been. Silent tears of grief tracked along her face into her pillow well into the night until she finally drifted off to the rhythmic breathing beside her.

Chapter Five

Nick spent much of the night dozing rather than sleeping. The strange bed, his earlier anger and worry at finding her door unlocked with her vulnerable on the couch when he'd come back, Maggie's stifled tears she was obviously trying to hide—all conspired to keep him on edge and made it difficult to let go and fall asleep.

He'd debated with himself earlier, finally caving after a trip home to unpack. He'd wanted to make sure Maggie was going to be all right. She'd looked so alone, so lost when he'd left, without the chance for any goodbyes between them. Then when he had returned, he'd been able to look right in and see her sleeping on the couch from the window in the front of the house. She was barefooted but had her jacket on, as though she hadn't had a chance to change into clean, comfortable clothes. Curled up on her side, hugging herself, she looked small and extremely vulnerable.

Some instinct had made him check the door before ringing the bell, and sure enough, it had been completely unlocked. Fear and anger had driven him inside to clear and secure the house. When he thought of what he'd seen happen to women, even those who took every precaution…

She'd even slept through his moving around, her only reaction to curl more tightly in on herself as he'd stood over her vulnerable form and watched. The thought of someone committing a crime of opportunity looming over her and doing the same had almost made him physically ill.

He thought he'd done an admirable job of fighting back his ire when he'd taken her up to bed, and indeed, now that she was safe and tucked away, he could focus on how to impress upon her the real need to be extra safe now that she would be living alone.

Nick frowned as he thought about that. From what he'd observed as he'd moved through the house, there was little evidence a man even lived here. Oh, there was a jacket and a couple of pairs of shoes he'd seen, and there were family pictures featuring a slight, blond man with glasses, along with a cute little girl with her mother's eyes and curls, only blonde like her dad. But that was it.

Maggie moved in her sleep, and he remembered her grip on his wrist, her eyes steady on his as she'd asked him to stay. Pleased to have the chance to talk to her, to maybe even become friends, he'd been more than happy to stay. She didn't imply anything untoward, although there had been a moment when he'd shucked his jeans off…

Although he hadn't been able to make out her exact expression in the dark, he'd felt the crackle of desire as something changed in the way she'd looked at him, held herself, maybe her breathing. But then, like a faucet turning off, it was gone, and she'd hunched away from him on the bed. Moments later, a hitch in her breath had given away her tears, even though she'd obviously tried to be silent. It was one of the hardest things he'd ever done, to leave her alone in that moment, only lending the tacit support of his presence, when all he'd wanted was to pull her into his arms and tell her everything was going to be fine.

She'd lost her husband. Things were a long way from being fine for her.

And she was a long way from wanting anything more than a warm body, someone at her side to keep it from being too quiet. Nick figured he was being used—oh, not in a bad way necessarily—as a substitute for the companion she was accustomed to. And that was fine. If it gave her some comfort, he could be whatever she needed. In a ridiculously short amount of time, she'd somehow twined her way into his heart. He didn't believe in love at first sight, but he knew chemistry when he felt it. Allowed to grow, love could come.

But that kind of growth was not in the foreseeable future.

Nick grimaced. *Figures.*

Ah well, he'd take what he could get. He had nothing but time. And speaking of which…

He lifted partway up and glanced at the clock. Nearly two a.m. He flopped back down and tried to blank his mind, then gave up and carefully rose from the bed. After quietly pulling his cell from his jeans pocket, he made his way downstairs to the living room. He dialed the desk and, as he suspected, got Rollie.

"Hey, Rollie, it's Nick."

"Nick! You back?"

"Yeah, just got in this afternoon."

"How was your grandma?"

"It was a good visit. She's getting up there, but still really active. Hey, can you look something up for me?"

"Sure, whatcha need?"

Nick gave Rollie Wade's name and the fact he'd been in an auto accident. "Might not be down as a fatality, though. I think he died at St Vincent's."

There was the sound of typing and a period of silence. "Okay, yeah. Another driver crossed into oncoming traffic. Three-car accident, four people transported. The driver at fault was dead on scene. Um, what else? No one under the influence. He— Wade Winters—had a clean driving record. Highway Patrol notified ex-wife Margaret Winters yesterday by phone. Do you need the number?"

Ex-wife? "Sure, go ahead."

Rollie gave him the number and Nick entered it into his phone. "That all you need, Nick? When are you back on shift?"

"Days, tomorrow... Uh, today."

"Well, damn, get some sleep then."

"Will do. Thanks, Rollie."

Nick hung up and finished entering Maggie's name on her contact page. They hadn't been married anymore. But Nick could swear she'd referred to Wade as her husband, not ex-husband. And she was still wearing her ring.

Huh. Well, maybe she just hadn't moved on yet, even though she was free. A sense of relief spread through him at the knowledge that instead of being attracted to a raw widow of a day's time, he was more acceptably interested in a divorced woman who had just lost her ex—which was bad enough. The other had just been disturbing. He blew out a breath, feeling much better about himself.

After one more check to make sure they were locked up, he headed upstairs then carefully got back into the far side of her bed. Settling in, actually feeling like he could rest this time, he realized part of his restlessness before was his subconscious unease at being in the bed of another man, in place of him. Letting go of that worry, he confirmed that his cell phone alarm was set and finally let himself relax into sleep.

* * * *

Maggie woke up slowly from a good dream that was getting better by the minute. She was tucked securely against a large male frame, her head pillowed on a muscular shoulder. There was no confusion, no mistaken identity. She knew instantly it was Nick — Wade had never been a cuddler, and moreover, Nick likely had at least fifty pounds on her ex.

The grief tried to intrude at the thought of Wade, and she pushed it away, purposely concentrating on the now. Her leg was thrown possessively across Nick, and she couldn't help a little movement, rubbing against his hair-roughened thigh. He squeezed her in response, and she smiled against his skin.

He'd stayed.

And had been a gentleman.

Not sure if she was truly happy with that or not, she wiggled a bit closer. His chest started to shake under her and, startled, she lifted her head to look at him, to find the movement was apparently stifled laughter. His eyes danced with amusement, and she frowned in response.

"What's so funny?"

He used his large hand to tuck her head back down against his shoulder. "You are. You sleep like the dead, but you're very wiggly when you wake up."

Her head popped back up as soon as he let go. She wanted to see him, but she had no desire to move anything else. *In fact...* She shifted her leg over his again, and he groaned, his head going back onto the pillow.

"Quit moving!"

A rush of pure feminine power overtook Maggie. It was as if she were another woman—a confident, sexy woman, certain of her own appeal. Trying not to think too much about what she was doing, she went on instinct instead. From the position she was in, it took about two seconds for Maggie to be straddling Nick.

From her new vantage point astride her sexy bed mate, she could see the surprise in his gaze being overtaken by heat.

"This isn't the best time for this," he cautioned, even as his hands came up to bracket her hips, holding her in place. "You need time."

"I need this. And there is no better time. We're here—now. The rest of the world can wait a while."

Nick's lips parted as if to argue, but then he gave her a wry grin instead. "You sound very certain."

"I am," Maggie agreed, needing to make it clear to him. "I'm not stupid. I know this is probably some knee-jerk, cycle of grief thing. But oh, I want this." She circled her hips against the growing erection beneath her, and he helped by holding her even more firmly and moving her exactly how he wanted.

He gave her a jerk forward, and she lost her balance, falling to catch herself on her elbows just above his shoulders. Now she was pressed against him from groin to chest. Her breasts were flattened against the hard wall of his upper torso. Her new angle had his cock rubbing against her clit on every pass as they rocked against one another, the two thin layers of their underwear no barrier to the heat and moisture being produced. Each thrust sent shockwaves of sensation through her, traveling from her pussy to her now-aching breasts and back to concentrate at her core.

Her lips parted. There wasn't enough oxygen in the world just then. Pulling back enough so the taut tips of her breasts just brushed against his solid chest, she lingered a breath above his lips. Their eyes locked and the kiss she craved was just an inch away. Maggie knew Nick wouldn't be the one to take it, that he would let her set the pace, and that made her even more determined to tempt him into making a move.

Maggie licked her lips as her gaze dropped to his mouth. His tongue was just visible inside his parted lips and she could feel the warmth of his breath on her face. She alternately surged with and fought against his hold on her hips, seeking the most contact she could, using her lower body to shamelessly stroke against his rigid erection.

This is the best sex I've had in my life, and we're still dressed.

Time to make it better.

Maggie sat up abruptly and pulled the T-shirt over her head in one swift movement. Nick's gasp ended in a growl as his patience finally broke. He tossed her off him onto the other side of the bed, and before she'd stopped bouncing, he had hold of her panties and pulled them down her legs.

He tossed the garment aside and deliberately slowed his movements as he worked the T-shirt over his head. At the first sight of his broad, muscled chest, Maggie forgot all about lying there naked and exposed.

Eagerly trailing her eyes over his form, she propped herself up on an elbow and followed the path of her gaze with her hand, all the way down to the waistband of the boxer briefs that had drawn her attention earlier that night. Her fingers slid just inside the elastic, and she began to pull downwards. Nick gave a heart-stopping little shimmy of assistance and she worked the last barrier downwards to his thighs as he rid himself of his shirt and used the freed hands to help push down his underwear then shifted to get them off his legs.

His erection hung long and thick—and Nick was uncircumcised. Distracted by the difference, she reached out before she could think and took him in hand. He hissed in a breath and pulsed against her palm.

"Wow," Maggie voiced her admiration and was gratified when Nick flushed red. "Can I...? Um..." She wasn't sure how to voice her request to explore and satisfy her curiosity about his foreskin. So instead, she stroked him and watched as the glistening red head emerged.

"Girl, you're killing me. Do whatever you want."

Maggie snorted. "Girl? I'm no girl." She kept up her slow stroking, mesmerized, until a bead of pre-cum welled in his slit. She inhaled and looked up.

Nick's heavy-lidded expression did crazy things to her insides and her pussy was literally clenching in anticipation.

I actually want *him to fuck me*, she thought, stunned.

Her sense that another person had taken over her body increased at the alien thought. But sure enough, all the signs were there. She mentally pictured herself as she was at that moment—sprawled before him, naked, breasts peaked and her folds moist, with her hand on his erect cock. Not a position she ever thought she'd be in, especially with a relative stranger.

But not one I'm going to squander either.

Chapter Six

Fighting through the feeling of her hand on him, which was still caressing him with a maddeningly light touch, Nick retained enough sense to see the acceptance in her eyes. But he still needed the words.

"Maggie?" He waited until he had her attention. "I won't do anything you don't want. We can stop anytime. We can stop right now. As little or as much as you want. Your call."

She didn't hesitate. "I don't want to stop."

He leaned down until he was braced over her. "What *do* you want?"

At the direct question, she opened her mouth then closed it. Her hands came up and ran along his lats then down to cup his ass in a firm grip. Her pressure pulled him forward enough so his cock rode against the softness of her belly.

"Would it be easier to answer what you *don't* want?" he tried one last time.

Her eyes shone up at him even in low light cast by the streetlamp, still on outside. She arched beneath him, seemingly seeking greater contact.

"I don't want to stop feeling like this."

At the heartfelt admission, he relented and lowered his body on top of hers, relishing the feel of her cradling him against her smooth skin. "How do you feel?" he murmured.

Maggie mouthed his jaw line, and he felt the tip of her tongue come out to taste him. He in turn let his own lips glide down the curve of her neck. She brought her legs up to wrap around the back of his, twining them together until they were completely aligned. One small movement would put him right where he was dying to be. He gritted his teeth, the effort to keep this two-way seduction slow straining every bit of patience he had.

"I feel...sexy. Hungry. Alive..." This last trailed off and he saw a hint of reality enter her expression. Waiting to see if it would be the tipping point, he nearly held his breath until she continued.

"I love feeling this way. It makes me think I've missed a lot in my life. I want you to show me."

There was no reply he could give that seemed adequate to answer the trust and responsibility she was asking him for. So instead, he tried to illustrate without words how vibrant and gorgeous he found her. Dipping his head, he took those small, tight nipples one at a time into his mouth, teething and tugging at them until they were standing at attention. Satisfied with her response, he tasted his way down her stomach, his frequent glances up at her rapt face spurring him onwards to the dark triangle protecting her core.

Shouldering her legs even farther apart, Nick found her pussy lips were partially spread and glistening. He ran his tongue through her folds, opening her completely, tasting her as she fought to ride his mouth. He stilled her hips with his hands, and suckled and lapped at her clit and dipped his tongue into her entrance.

Her moans and cries intensified until at once, she arched up against him and he tongued her through her climax, pulling back only when her hands scrabbled at his shoulders. Loving the feel of her dampness on his lips and chin, he moved upwards to share her taste in a long, lush kiss that left them both panting.

Absolutely at the breaking point, he pulled back reluctantly and slid to the side of the bed in order to reach for his pants.

"What? Where are you going?" Maggie's voice sounded almost panicked as she sat up quickly. Not wanting to cause her a moment of worry, he turned to soothe her with a kiss.

"Just getting some protection, sweetheart."

"Oh." Her chagrined tone made him ache for her.

"It's no reflection on you or on me. It's just smart, a precaution."

"Of course, I know that. I just didn't think." She rolled her eyes, self-deprecatingly, and Nick relaxed and grinned. After pulling a condom from his wallet, he opened it, then held her eyes with his own as he gave his shaft a few hard pumps before placing the disc at the tip.

Her expression abruptly changed as she watched him hold and roll the condom down his length, and her admiring gaze made him even harder. When was the last time he'd ever been regarded with such blatant yet innocent interest? Nick shook his head. Nothing about Maggie was like anything he'd ever experienced before, from her wide-eyed reactions to her sultry siren song. His protectiveness toward her was yet another new sensation.

He laid her back and stroked her warmth with his fingers, testing her readiness, then removed his touch and sank his sheathed cock into her welcoming folds. Her gasp echoed his as they came together and he paused to allow her to adjust. Damn, she was tight. She was a petite little thing, and he also wagered it had been a while. Rocking side to side instead of the further penetration he was aching for, he tried to give her time to become accustomed to his presence.

Then she took matters into her own hands, so to speak, by trailing her fingertips down his pecs to his nipples and giving them a caress. Always a hot spot for him, he couldn't keep from thrusting in reflex, finally sinking all the way into her.

That thrust felt so good, and Maggie had nothing but desire and want in her eyes, so he began to move. The slow, rhythmic pace he set effectively edged his impending climax — all the time spent in such close proximity to her, sleeping with her, the foreplay — it all had kept him at the breaking point for longer than he'd thought possible.

Nick finally let his body take over, his penetration going deeper and harder until sweat trickled down his back and temples. Maggie was a quiet, wordless lover, but the gasps and moans deep in her throat gave him all the feedback he needed.

He got a hand between them and thrummed her hard clit along with his thrusts and she went wild beneath him, finally arching against him as he rode her to his own finish. The squeeze of her passage on his shaft at the peak of its sensitivity prolonged his pleasure. "Ah, babe. Maggie," he called then, his strength fading, he rolled to his side, taking her with him.

Holding her close, their damp skin pressed together and breaths comingling, he rested his forehead against hers. Her dark lashes rested against her pale skin, and he closed his own eyes as well. After a few minutes, he was forced to disentangle himself and grasp the condom as he slipped from her body.

After a trip to the bathroom to take care of necessities, he returned to find Maggie curled on her side away from him. A twinge of foreboding hit him at the tell-tale body language.

She stiffened as he slipped back in behind her. Ignoring her silent protest, he pulled her back against his chest and decided to take the bull by the horns.

"What's going through your mind, Maggie?"

After a moment, a shrug was her only response and his sense of dread grew.

"Talk to me. What's wrong?"

"What's wrong?" she asked incredulously, and the strain in her voice made him wince. She turned over to face him, tears streaking down her face. "What could possibly be wrong? My daughter's father is dead, and I have a funeral to plan, and here I am, rolling around in my bed with some...kid." She sat up, grabbed the sheet and tucked it firmly in place under her arms.

Defensiveness boiled up in Nick, even as he recognized Maggie was just striking out in her guilt and grief. "Can I remind you that I told you this wasn't the best time for this? That I asked you, repeatedly, if you were sure this was what you wanted? I gave you every opportunity to stop."

"Of course you did, but you knew I wouldn't. You had me so turned on—" She cut off abruptly.

"You asked me to continue. I gave you control of the situation at every possible stopping point. I did *not* take advantage of you," he gritted, even as he owned up to himself that it was possible he *had*. What had he been thinking? He should have known this would be the outcome. He should have been the clear-headed one.

Remorse filled him and his anger deflated. "Ah, Maggie, I'm sorry. I honestly thought this was what you wanted. I thought you enjoyed it."

Her face crumpled. "I *did*." Then she was sobbing, and he understood. She was upset because she *had* enjoyed it, had wanted it, and was beating herself up for being human.

He took her in his arms, and while she was still stiff, she didn't pull away. "Shhh," he tried to soothe, wishing he knew what to do or say to take away her pain.

"I feel horrible. Just horrible. What kind of person am I?"

"A human one," he tried to make her see. "There's nothing wrong about needing comfort, or something to take your mind off things. It's been a very stressful, painful time, and you have so much more ahead of you. Don't blame yourself" —*or me*— "for trying to alleviate that pressure for a little while. C'mon, it's okay. Shhh…"

Nick rocked her in his arms a while and she gave herself over to his care, crying herself limp. Finally easing her back down to the pillow, he was about to lie down and join her when his cell phone's alarm intruded into the quiet.

Maggie gasped and Nick cursed as he fumbled for the phone on the bedside table and turned it off.

He turned back toward her. "Sorry about that. I'm on days today."

The tone of her voice was calm and distant, and she didn't meet his gaze. "It's okay. Go ahead. You can use my shower if you want."

His heart ached at the divide she was erecting between them. It was as if he was losing something precious just as he'd discovered it. "Hey." She kept her eyes averted. They were puffy but dry now, and in a way, it was worse than the tears had been. "Please look at me for a sec."

Maggie finally looked up, and he could see the resolve in her expression. Changing what he was going to say, he asked, "Do you need me to do anything before I go? Or after my shift?"

She shook her head. "No. I have my friend coming over. I'll be fine."

There didn't seem to be much more to say. He gathered his clothing and gun and dressed, then tucked away his wallet and phone in his jeans. On second thought, he pulled out his wallet and extracted a department business card. Looking around, he spotted a pen on the writing desk across the room, then grabbed it and jotted down his personal numbers and email. "Here's how you can get hold of me. Call me if you need anything, or if you even just want to chat. Okay?"

She sat there on the bed, tucked up in her sheet, looking very small and vulnerable with her shoulders bare and hair tousled. But there was steel in her expression—not necessarily directed at him but at trying to keep herself together. The only thing left for him to put on was his footwear, and he knew in a minute he'd have no excuse left to keep him here.

"Nick?"

He paused in sliding his last shoe on.

"Thank you. For tonight. Well, for everything."

"My pleasure." There was absolute sincerity in that response right now. He knew, though, that he'd be thinking about the real pleasure they'd shared for days and nights to come. "Take care, Maggie."

"You too."

He straightened. "I'll meet you downstairs if you want to grab a robe or something. I don't want to leave until you're there to lock up behind me." Nick dropped his gaze to her mouth and she parted her lips. Lips he wanted to kiss and be damned with the consequences.

He strode from the room and waited impatiently downstairs for the few minutes it took her to descend. The sight of her slight frame bundled up in her plush robe, bare feet peeking out from beneath the hem, made him wish foolishly that she could send him off to work every morning just like this.

She stunned him by following him to the door and hugging him from behind as he reached to unlock it. He froze, not wanting to spook her, confused yet pleased by her initiative. He felt her press her cheek or temple to the middle of his back, and couldn't resist reaching around behind him to give her an awkward sort of reverse hug in return.

"I'm sorry I'm running so hot and cold right now," she murmured.

He tried to get a sense of her mood, but it was difficult without seeing her expressive face. As much as he was enjoying her platonic embrace, he wanted to see her eyes. He eased himself out of her slightly resisting arms then immediately turned and pulled her into a true, hard hug before setting her away from him, keeping his hands clasping her upper arms.

"I would be surprised if you were taking all of this in stride. I just want you to be okay, and not to beat yourself up over what's happening between us." He used present tense on purpose, because as far as he was concerned, he didn't want to walk away from her. Sometime during the night, his mind had been made up. She might need some time and distance, but he wasn't giving up on her completely. He could be the friend she needed now and hope for more later.

By her thoughtful, wary expression she hadn't missed his choice of words. "Nick," she began, "I'm so not ready—"

"I know," he interrupted, not wanting her to build up a head of steam and decide to cut things off completely. "I completely understand. You may think I'm young, but I'm not some kid who needs immediate gratification, Maggie. I want to be your friend. Maybe sometime down the road we can look at things differently, but no pressure, okay? Let's just see what happens. You need to focus on yourself and your daughter right now—I get that."

Maggie gave him a wry smile he hadn't been expecting. "Sounds like you're cutting off every one of my arguments at the knees." She shifted a bit and he glanced down at her bare feet again, which had to be getting cold with her standing on the tile.

"You must be chilled. You should have put on the slippers I saw by your bed. Come on." He took her hand and pulled her over into the carpeted living room. He sat on the couch then tugged her down next to him. She immediately tucked her legs to the side, covering her feet with the hem of her robe.

"You're right. I hadn't noticed how cold I was getting until just then." Maggie sighed and glanced at him. "You're very observant."

"A bit, yes." Nick knew he needed to come clean about checking into Wade's death. "And sometimes when I don't know something I do research. I made a call last night—just wanted to check the details on the accident. I hope you're not upset."

Maggie frowned slightly then shrugged as her expression cleared. "No, not really. I pretty much told you everything I know."

Nick forged ahead, wanting to get everything out in the open. "I learned that you're actually Wade's ex-wife."

Her lips parted then a slight blush crept up her neck. She cleared her throat. "Well, about that..." She paused and he waited patiently. "I guess I did give you the impression that our marriage was current, but it wasn't my conscious intention to mislead you at first. It honestly still just slips out in the present tense sometimes, and takes more explanation than I want to get into to set the facts straight. Especially with people I don't know." She seemed fascinated by the end of her belt, toying with it and keeping her gaze downward. "Plus, I kind of felt like I needed the boundary between us. So I didn't clarify. But Wade and I—we were together since before we knew what sex was. And we're still friends, plus he still stays here at the house to be with Cass sometimes." Maggie pressed her lips together. "I mean stayed." She swallowed hard. "It was hard enough to think of him in the past tense when we were divorced, and now..."

Nick hugged her tightly to him. "I understand." After a few moments where she willingly rested in his embrace, he eased her upright then stood. "I'm sorry. I really have to get going to work. Can I call you later?"

"You don't have to..."

"I want to. Okay? Like I said—friends. No pressure. I just want to check in and do what I can. Is that all right?" Nick gazed at her and tried to make sure his sincerity showed in his eyes. She gave a slight nod, and he relaxed. "Good. I'll give you a ring when I get off shift tonight, but if you need anything before then, you can call me on my cell. The number's on the card I gave you."

He reached down and tugged her to her feet. "Come lock up behind me, please." Frowning, he recalled the night before. "And make sure to keep it locked when you're here in the house alone. I just walked right in last night and you slept right through it. Someone could have really—"

"I know." She reached up and pressed her fingers to his mouth to cut him off. "I usually do. I promise."

Her touch sent a tingle through him, but he knew he'd be pressing his luck to act on it. He settled for giving her a quick kiss on the forehead. "Take care, and call if you need me."

Maggie nodded, but he got the impression she was humoring him. He didn't push.

Once he walked out, he waited pointedly until he heard the distinct sound of the deadbolt engaging before giving a wave at the peephole then striding toward his SUV. He'd parked on the opposite side of the street rather than in her driveway, not wanting to set her neighbors to talking if they were the type to do so—especially since he'd still thought she'd been freshly widowed when he'd come back to check on her the night before.

Before he crossed the street, he looked back at the house and saw her watching him through the window. His spirits lifted and he gave another wave, this time seeing her return it. He walked to his car feeling much better about where things had been left and hoping to hear from her later on.

Chapter Seven

Maggie glanced at her phone on the seat next to her when a text notification sounded. Sam's contact photo smiled up at her.

I'm coming by with some dinner for you. Do you want Champ back or me to keep him?

She thought about that for a minute. It would definitely make the house seem less empty tonight when she went to bed, but then again, she would probably be flying back to Mom's in a couple of days. It probably wasn't fair to him to have him come home then send him away again.

A few minutes later she pulled into her driveway and idled there for a minute while she pressed the garage door opener then answered the text.

Probably better to stay there until we're back from Mom's. Thanks for checking. See you soon.

She drove into the garage and parked, then sat there listening to the engine ticking. With a sigh, she glanced at, then disregarded the bag of Wade's effects from the hospital and the huge folder of paperwork from the funeral home, letting it all stay in the car while she got out and closed up behind her.

As she did so, she thought about Nick—not for the first time by a long shot. Her long emotional day had alternately been made easier and more difficult as flashes from her time with him popped into her head at random intervals.

It had been a grueling day and one she was glad to have over with. There had only been two things she hadn't got done that she'd wanted to—checking on Wade's apartment and stopping at the auto shop. His apartment could wait for another time, she figured, sometime when she wasn't so bone-weary and heartsick. And the visit to the shop had turned out to be unnecessary once she'd checked. Since the car had been totaled, all of the claims could be handled over the phone. There hadn't been any surviving personal belongings that she'd wanted, either, so she'd been able to skip that altogether. Probably a good thing since she really didn't have any desire to see the wrecked vehicle and imagine Wade inside.

Maggie shuddered and dropped her purse on the kitchen counter then ran a hand through her hair. She rolled her neck, wondering if she should make herself some coffee. Part of her wasn't looking forward to Sam's visit, only because she was exhausted and would rather just shut everything down. But Sam was the only person she really couldn't say no to—Sam knew her so well and always seemed to have her best interests at heart. Like tonight, for example. It was just like her to announce that she was bringing dinner by because she would know that Maggie had gone through the whole day without eating. And once there, Maggie knew Sam would listen to her vent if needed, stay until the words ran out, then give her back her privacy without overstaying her welcome.

She gave in to temptation and started brewing a cup of coffee with her single-cup machine. She glanced at the house phone and noticed the message light blinking. Purposely turning her back on it, needing a break from the constant calls, even those from friends and extended family, she went about fixing her drink then grabbed her cell phone and wandered into the living room.

As she settled on the couch, she thought back to that morning when she'd sat with Nick in almost the same position she was in now. A small part of her was a bit disappointed that he hadn't called her today, though… She cocked her head as she wondered, did he even have her phone number? That was probably why he'd given her his numbers and said for her to call him. That, and leaving the decision to make contact ever again up to her.

She took a sip from her brimming mug before she spilled any then set it down on the coffee table. Glancing at the wall clock, she figured with the time change that Mom and Cass would be done with dessert and probably watching a movie. Good time to get the goodnight call done. Maggie settled back and dialed.

"Hi!"

The sound of her daughter's voice was both a balm and heartbreaking at the same time. She inhaled sharply through her nose to try to control her sudden emotions. "Hi, baby. Is your grandma around?"

"Of course she is, where else would she be? Guess what we did today? We went shopping today and had lunch at that Chinese buffet place. Oh my God, I ate so much. I had, like, thirds and then you know how they have that dessert bar?"

"Mm-hmm…" Her daughter's exuberant rambling lifted her spirits. Relaxing, she reached for her mug then tucked her legs up to side and leaned into the corner of the couch.

"So I had to have a dish of the twist ice cream, of course, but they also had éclairs and…"

Maggie sipped her drink and lost herself in the fairly one-sided conversation with Cass for a few minutes as she excitedly filled Maggie in on her day. Her coffee mug was about half empty when Cassie asked, "How's Champ?"

"I haven't seen him, honey. He's still at Auntie Sam's since I'll be coming back there in a couple of days."

"Oh good. I miss you. I mean, I'm having fun with Grandma, but it's kinda weird without you here. Why did you have to go home anyway?"

Maggie's breath caught. They hadn't said anything to Cass about the accident, wanting to wait until they knew more before mentioning it. Then Wade had died…

She purposely kept her answer vague and brief. "To do something I had to be in Oregon for. Is Grandma handy? Sam's coming over soon and I'd like to talk to her before she gets here."

Thankfully, Cassie didn't push. "Okay, yeah, she's right here. Goodnight, Mom. Tell Sam to hug Champ for me."

"Will do, baby. Goodnight."

There was a pause and a murmur then her mom came on the line. "Hi, honey."

"Hey, Mom." That awful wave of emotion came back at the sound of her mother's voice. "How are things going?"

"We're just fine. No need to worry yourself. More importantly, how are things there?" Maggie heard the tell-tale squeak of the door into her mom's garage opening and knew she'd walked out to give them some privacy. "Did you have to go to the hospital?"

"Just briefly to pick up his wallet and a few other things." She'd asked them to get rid of his clothes. "I didn't have to…see him, only sign the release for the funeral home to take possession of…him." 'The body' was what she'd started to say. Such bizarre and distant language. "Then I went there to figure out my options. He wanted to be cremated, of course, so that's simpler. And I want to wait on the service. It doesn't have to be right away."

"That's true. You don't want to put it off too long, though."

Maggie nodded. She knew it would weigh on her to have it looming in the distance. And probably better for Cass too, to have it soon then move on. God knew, the grieving process was going to be long and hard for all of them, but especially poor Cass. Maggie gave up on trying to not cry and she sniffled a bit as the tears finally overflowed her brimming eyes and ran down both cheeks.

"Oh, Maggie. I'm so sorry, honey. I hate that you're alone. I wish I could be there with you to help you." Her mom sounded on the brink of tears herself.

"You are, Mom, just by being with Cass and letting me do some of the work before I have to break it to her. And I'm not completely alone. I have good friends here." Nick popped into her mind. "Like Sam, who should be here any minute."

"All right. I'll let you go. You be careful, staying there by yourself, okay?"

"Yes, Mom." Despite her sad mood, she smiled, thinking that Nick and her mom were alike in their protectiveness.

"When do you think you'll be coming back?"

Maggie thought about what she had to do. "My ticket's flexible, so whenever I can find an open flight. I've only got a few more small things to do in person here, and the rest can either be done over the phone or can wait until we come back. I can probably wrap things up tomorrow, so day after tomorrow maybe. I'll let you know when I book it."

"Okay. Get some rest. And don't forget to eat."

"I won't. Sam's bringing over something for dinner," she mentioned, knowing that would help satisfy her mom's worry.

"Good."

Maggie had to smile at her mom's predictability. "I'm going to let you go. Kiss Cass for me. And we'll talk soon."

"Night, honey."

"Goodnight." Maggie disconnected and set down her phone on the side table with a deep breath and exhale. She felt badly about prevaricating to Cass, but telling her something so huge over the phone was out of the question. It left her feeling out of sorts, though, and her mind was spinning.

God, I wish I could just…

Just what? She wasn't sure. But the memory of Nick's strong, comforting presence slipped into her head and went a long way toward soothing her. She looked at her phone. Of course, his number wasn't in it. His card was on her nightstand upstairs where she'd left it that morning, so she couldn't act on the urge to call him, to hear his deep, sympathetic voice, to ask him to come over…

A sound at the front door brought her back to the present and she turned just in time to see Sam letting herself in with her key.

"Hi, sweetheart." Sam's face was pale and tight with emotion, and Maggie rose to meet her friend in a lingering half-hug since one arm was full. Of course it would be difficult for her too. She'd been one of the first friends Maggie had made when she and Wade had moved to Oregon, so Sam had known him just as long as she'd known Maggie. Sam's husband Chris was friends with Wade, though the families didn't get together quite as often since the divorce. Maggie briefly wondered how Chris was handling things, then tried to tune the thought out. She barely had enough emotional energy to handle herself and her family right now without worrying about everyone else.

Maggie had tears in her eyes but her cheeks were dry when she pulled back from Sam. "Here, let me take that." She took the brown paper takeout bag from Sam's arm and led the way into the kitchen.

"I got Chinese. I figured that's one kind of food you can eat even when you don't have an appetite." Sam set down a plastic sack with drinks in it, by the sounds of it. She sniffed then frowned. "Did you just make coffee?"

"Yes, you want one?"

"Nah. I'll just have one of these Monsters."

Maggie raised her eyebrows. "You're gonna be up all night."

"It's early enough I don't think I'll have a problem. Besides, you're one to talk, drinking coffee," Sam pointed out with a smile then sobered. "Are you okay? I have to say, you look better than I thought you would."

Maggie thought about it for the time it took to retrieve her drink from the living room. "I'm okay for now. I think I was able to work through a lot of the initial impact during the trip home and last night." Her cheeks went hot as she recalled just what it was she had done upstairs the night before. She coughed once into her hand then continued, "The tough part's going to be with Cass. And probably the memorial, and going through Wade's things... I guess all sorts of stuff, but mostly Cass. It's hard to know how she'll deal with it down the road, but she's going to be devastated when I tell her."

Sam nodded sympathetically. "She loves her daddy." She grimaced. "Sorry."

"What for, hon?"

"I don't know, actually. It's just really hard." Sam teared up and Maggie put an arm over her shoulders. It was somewhat ironic, but probably helpful in a way, that Maggie was in the role of comforter rather than the one being emotional for a change. "I mean, I know it's a million times harder for you, of course, but I just keep thinking..." She paused and inhaled sharply through her nose.

"You keep thinking what if it happened to Chris," Maggie guessed, correctly if Sam's fresh tears were any indication.

"I'm sorry. I don't mean to make it about me." Sam pulled away and dashed at her cheeks with the back of her hand. She went purposefully to the carryout bag and started pulling out white containers. "I got a few different things because I wasn't sure what you were in the mood for."

Maggie recognized Sam's need to distract herself with busywork, and far from being miffed that Sam was feeling fragile, she was a bit relieved that she wouldn't be encouraged to recount the whole situation and her feelings over and over. She could use a break.

Once they had all the food opened up and had dished out platefuls, they moved to the kitchen table and began eating in relative silence. Sam attacked the food like she hadn't eaten for days—not surprising, since she tended to be an emotional eater. Luckily she had a great metabolism for a woman their age. Maggie tended to lean in the other direction, losing her appetite when upset, so she was pleased to realize after the first couple of token bites that she was actually hungry. She finished off a helping of spicy shrimp with rice, then ate a couple of potstickers before setting her chopsticks down and sipping her coffee. Probably tea would have gone better, but she didn't want to bother with it.

Sam finally slowed down and popped up to start clearing the food away.

"Just leave it—I'll get to it later. Come in and sit with me."

Sam began to protest, but Maggie walked out of the kitchen into the living room. There were the sounds of a flurry of activity in the kitchen including the fridge door opening and closing a couple of times, and within a few minutes Sam had joined Maggie in the living room.

She plopped down next to Maggie on the couch and ran her hand through her very short blonde hair. "I don't know how you're not a complete mess," she stated bluntly.

"I'm not sure either. But I was yesterday. Crying all over —" Maggie cut herself off abruptly. She'd been about to mention Nick, but she really didn't want to go there right then. Not that she was worried her friend would think less of her...though who knew how Sam would react, especially since she was so grief-stricken over the loss of Wade?

Sam didn't seem to notice her little stumble. "I'm sure. You had to have been going crazy on the flight home. I'm sorry I didn't pick up when you called — I think I was working out."

Maggie shrugged, trying to look casual. "It was hard, but kind of peaceful too." Sam looked at her expectantly. More seemed to be needed, so she continued, "In a way, it was good to have the time to start to process it before I got back and had to dive right in. And I had a really nice seatmate who was very understanding." That was an understatement.

"Oh no. Not one of those. Did they ever leave you alone? I hate the ones who just keep talking and talking to you."

"I know what you mean, but it wasn't like that at all. He was a really great guy." She knew she probably sounded defensive but couldn't help but stick up for Nick.

"He was, was he?" Sam gave her a probing look. "And where exactly did Mr Wonderful fall on the rating scale?" Maggie shrugged but Sam seized onto the topic like a dog with a bone. "Oh my God, are you blushing?"

Waving a hand at her persistent friend, Maggie willed her cheeks to cool. "He was..." Ready to assign him to a somewhat plausible ranking like Total Stud, she found she just couldn't lie. "Off the charts," she admitted.

"Did you get a picture?"

"Sam!"

"Well?"

Maggie shook her head. "No…" She cringed, knowing instantly that giving her intuitive friend anything but a decisive 'no' was a big mistake.

As she'd predicted, Sam pounced on the open-ended answer. "You didn't get a picture, but it sounds like you got something, Margaret Jean."

Maggie felt like her face was about to explode. She was really going to have to work on her evasiveness skills. Silence was her only ally now.

Her cell phone ringing broke their standoff and she half rose then stopped indecisively. What if it was Nick? She didn't want to take his call in front of her friend.

Sam showed no such compunctions and headed rapidly for the kitchen.

She wouldn't…

Eyes widening, Maggie pulled herself together and hurried after her.

"Hello? Maggie's phone."

She would. That witch.

"May I tell her who is calling?"

Maggie burst into the kitchen and her gaze collided with Sam's.

Her friend held out her cell phone. "It's…Nick." Her eyebrows went up so high they were practically in her hairline.

Maggie yanked the phone out of Sam's hand and took a deep breath. "Hello?"

"Hi there."

Nick's deep voice did crazy things to her insides, curling down from her chest to her still somewhat tender pussy, though she tried her best to hide her reaction from Sam.

"Hi," she managed, wondering how the hell she was supposed to be able to have a conversation with Sam there. Luckily, Nick was as in tune with her as ever.

"I understand that you have company right now, so it's probably not a good time to talk. I just wanted to check in with you and see if you needed me to come by this evening."

"Um..." *What to do?* "Yes," she heard herself replying then wondered what the hell she was thinking.

"Okay. I have to make a couple of stops first, so it'll be at least an hour. Have you eaten dinner?"

"Yes."

"Good. I'll see you in a little while. Bye, Maggie."

"Bye." She heard the call disconnect and set her phone down on the counter, then fiddled around plugging it into the charger to buy herself a little bit more time.

"Nick, huh? Was that Mr Off-the-Charts?"

Maggie shook her head slightly, not in denial of the question but just because she didn't want to get into it right now — not when things were so complicated and about a minute old. "Yes," she admitted. "He was just checking to see if I was doing okay." She wondered if Sam had been able to hear Nick's end of the conversation. Not much she could do about it if she had. It wasn't like she'd done anything wrong, per se. Just...out of character.

"Okay." Sam's acknowledgment was soft, and Maggie understood that her friend was backing off and giving her space. "He sounds like a nice guy."

"He is," she confirmed with a mental sigh.

"Well, I'm going to get back to the horde." Sam was suddenly in motion, gathering her purse and heading to the front door.

Maggie trailed along behind her, unsure of what to say. "Thanks for dinner." She watched as Sam slid her sandals on then gave her a quick hug.

"You're welcome. Get some rest. I'll call you tomorrow."

It was all everything Sam would normally say upon leaving, but there seemed to be a sort of deeper meaning to it all that Maggie couldn't quite confirm or puzzle out. Did she know something? Was she just guessing? Or was it all business as usual?

Only time would tell.

She closed the door behind Sam and locked it, knowing that it would be the first thing that Nick would check when he got there.

Nick is coming.

She was a grown woman in her forties with a daughter to raise on her own and a memorial to plan. Her breath shouldn't catch at the mere thought of a man she'd known for about a day's time.

Breath? What breath?

Chapter Eight

Nick couldn't help but test the front door, relieved when he found it locked tight. *Good girl*. He knocked and waited, listening as he heard a loud banging noise from somewhere above then what sounded like footsteps running down the stairs. He grinned at the thought of Maggie racing down to answer the door like a teenager.

There was a moment of quiet then he saw a change in the light behind the peephole before the deadbolt was disengaged. Maggie opened the door and though she gave Nick as smile as she stepped back to let him in, he could see the weariness beneath her effort at welcome. "Hi there. Come on in."

"Thanks for having me over."

"Oh, well, of course." Maggie's gaze slid away from his. He knew her discomfort was probably from the awkward dilemma of how to greet him. They were, after all, practically strangers, but also had intimate knowledge of each other.

Nick took over closing and locking the door behind him then made the decision for the both of them and folded her into a firm embrace. After a moment, she melted against him and slid her arms around his waist to hold him back. He had no desire to pull away, so they stood there in the foyer for a couple of minutes, with Nick trying to convey his support through the undemanding hug, trying to be there for her after what had to have been an extremely rough day.

"Did you get any sleep after I left this morning?" At his question, Maggie pulled back and he reluctantly released her. She looked a bit more at ease, though still tired.

"No, I stayed up. I had"—she blew out a breath and grimaced—"a lot to do today."

"And none of it easy, I imagine." He changed the subject when she didn't respond to that right away. She probably wasn't particularly anxious to revisit her day. "I had an interesting day. You know how when you take a vacation, then you come back and everything goes crazy?" He took a step further into the house, not trying to be presumptuous, but not sure she realized they were still standing in the entranceway.

He knew he'd guessed right when she rolled her eyes self-deprecatingly and gestured in the general direction of the kitchen. "Yes. Sorry. Why don't you come into the kitchen? I'll get you something to drink and you can tell me about it. Have you had any dinner yet? There's a ton of leftover Chinese." She was babbling slightly and he wasn't sure whether it was because she was nervous or tired.

He followed her into the kitchen and stood at the edge of the counter, not wanting to chance his weight on one of the rather small stools. Of course, if they'd been bought with her daughter in mind, no wonder they didn't look very sturdy. "I made myself a sandwich when I stopped at home to clean up."

Raising her eyebrows at him, she paused in front of the fridge. "Just a sandwich? That can't have been enough." She gave him a once-over and though he was sure it was innocent in the context of the conversation, he felt her gaze as though it was a physical touch. His body began to react predictably and he decided *the hell with it* and went ahead and chanced the seat. He released a thankful sigh as it held his weight, and moreover, now the counter shielded his partial erection from her view.

She apparently took him sitting down to mean that he was hungry after all, and started getting take-out boxes out of the fridge and setting them the counter in front of him. "Just dish what you want onto a plate and I'll warm it up. It'll be faster than heating them all separately." She laid a plate in front of him and handed him a couple of spoons from the drawer. "What would you like to drink?"

"Tea would be great if you have it. Just doesn't seem right to have anything else with Chinese." He began dishing what looked like Kung Pao beef onto his plate.

Maggie gave him a smile and moved to fill the kettle. "That's ironic. I had the same thought earlier, but I'd just made myself a coffee when Sam got here with the food." She set two mugs on the counter and pulled out an assortment of teas for him to choose from. He picked out a black tea and she followed suit, putting the rest away. "Here" — she took his packet from his hand — "I'll get these ready. You finish filling your plate."

When the tea was steeping and his food was warmed, she pulled down a small plate and dumped the rest of the potstickers onto it. He lifted an eyebrow in query and she shrugged with a smirk. "Love 'em and they'll go with my tea. Chopsticks or a fork?" She put her plate into the microwave.

"Chopsticks, of course." He grinned when she nodded sagely.

"Oh, of course." She got two nice, lacquered sets with stands out and put them on the counter, took her plate out then walked around to sit on the stool next to him.

It was nice, and oddly domestic, sitting there eating with her. He couldn't remember the last time he'd eaten at a counter, but of course she had a child, so they probably did so a lot, especially for quick meals.

He reached over and plucked a potsticker off her plate then popped it in his mouth.

"Hey!" She gaped at him. "I can't believe you just did that." The twinkle of humor in her eyes belied her exclamation.

"Sorry. It just called to me." The food was excellent, even warmed up, and he sighed appreciatively as he continued to eat. She'd been right—the quick, cold sandwich hadn't been enough, but he'd been in a hurry to get over here. "This is really good. Where's it from?"

"Lee's Kitchen."

"Oh, right—love that place. But I always get the Peking noodles. They're amazing, so I haven't really ventured into the rest of the menu."

She gave him a sidelong look then started toying with a potsticker. "So what happened today at work that made it crazy?"

He groaned and took a sip of tea before answering. "What didn't happen?"

"One of those days, huh?"

"Yeah." He shrugged. "It's like that. Sometimes it's quiet as hell. And other times you can't catch a break."

"It's not really dangerous, though, is it? I mean, in the suburbs."

He sobered and met her enquiring gaze at close range. "It may be the 'burbs. But even in affluent areas, there are still intense scenarios. And we're part of a large metro area." He put his chopsticks down and leaned back. "Which means some big-city problems can tend to spill over. But really, even if we were in a small town or the country, there are a lot of the same issues."

He thought how to answer her original question. Unfortunately, a lot of women—and men for that matter—couldn't handle the stress of being with a police officer. When he boiled it down, one way or another that had been the reason that every relationship he'd started had ended. His two longer-term relationships had both ended when his girlfriends had realized that, in essence, they didn't want to marry a cop, so why continue to date one? And the same factor had kept others from even trying past a date or two. Either that, or they were just in it to collect the badge then move on—more about what he did than who he was.

He shook off his disappointing recollections. "It can be dangerous, yes. I just have to be prepared in every situation and know how to react if things go bad."

She nodded somberly in response. "I guess I knew that. I just like to think that it's safer here, but..." Her mouth twisted.

"In many ways it is. You can't live your life in fear, Maggie. What you can do is take what precautions you can and realize that sometimes things happen that are out of your control or outside the norm, and decide how you'll handle it when they do." Nick reflected that a lot of what he'd just said could apply to the situation she now found herself in, but didn't point that out to her. She was a smart woman.

They were quiet for a minute before Maggie broke the silence. "It was a good reminder last night to keep my doors locked. It's unlikely someone would discover that fact, but why make it easy on them?"

"Exactly."

She clasped her hands in front of her. "Thanks for everything you've done."

A bit alarmed at how much that sounded like the prelude to a goodbye, Nick straightened in his seat. "You don't have to thank me. It was my pleasure."

His last word lingered in the air between them and the atmosphere seemed to thicken and spark, awareness zinging to life.

Maggie shifted then cocked her head to the side. "I want you to know I didn't ask you to come over for a booty call."

That unlikely phrase coming from her mouth caused Nick to choke on a laugh as he disbelievingly met her gaze. "No?" he managed.

"Well, I just…" She trailed off, her cheeks getting pinker by the second. But then she lifted her chin and met his eyes calmly as she continued, "I missed your company. I thought maybe we could talk?" It came out like a question. "Get to know each other. I mean, I know we talked for hours yesterday on the plane, but honestly, I was a bit out of it. Then last night… Anyway, do you mind? Just…chatting?"

There was something sweet and a bit poignant about her wanting to go back and fill in the blanks they'd rushed over in the unexpected coupling of the night before. She obviously wasn't the one-night-stand type, so her processing of last night was probably still ongoing. Nick didn't mind in the least that she wanted to spend time with him, and if that was all there was to it, that was absolutely fine with him.

A niggling, wary voice in the back of his head chattered at him that maybe she was protesting too much and that was why she'd come up with 'booty call' out of thin air—because that *was* why she'd invited him over. Either that or as a sort of security blanket.

He shoved the naysayer into the corner and closed the door. If that was what he could give to her, either a feeling of safety or physical comfort, so be it. At this point, he would give her whatever she asked for, whatever the end result happened to be, as long as it was of benefit to her.

"Sure, Maggie. Anything you want." Nick grinned at her and her mouth went dry. *Wow.* The guy was beautiful when he smiled like that. It was hard to believe he was single, but then again, he was relatively young. Probably still playing the field, and why not?

Maggie stood and he followed suit then she led the way out of the kitchen. As they passed the threshold, he subtly took charge of the situation and steered her toward the couch in the living room with a warm hand on the small of her back, just above her buttocks. Completely conscious of the movement of her curves beneath his hand as she walked, she had to force herself to breathe normally.

Anything you want...

His offhand comment had her brain running off in a direction she was quickly and shockingly becoming familiar with, and the hand on her back wasn't helping her think clearly at all. It was a long moment before she could even remember what she had wanted to ask. He slid his hand across her back, fingertips trailing off her hip as she sat, and he joined her on the couch, muscular arm draped casually behind her, his knee lolling heavily against her leg. Nick seemed to gravitate to her, was always touching her, and she soaked up the physical affection like a sponge.

"I was wondering…" Maggie paused as she caught herself lowering her hand to the muscular leg pressing against hers. Stopping the motion just in time, she couldn't quite figure out what to do. She paused with it hovering there for a second, then he made the decision for her as he laced their fingers together and dropped the joined hands to his thigh.

"Yes?" he said.

She met his eyes at close range, and the desire and acceptance she read there caused her breath to catch in her throat.

Seriously, Maggie, why are you fighting this?

She had no firm answer for herself, so she swayed forward and pressed her mouth gently against his parted lips, holding her breath for some reason, until she was forced to exhale with a gush. He had been completely still, watching her, but this seemed to be the signal he was waiting for and he seized control of the kiss, deepening the contact with a sleek tangling of tongues.

Nick pressed Maggie back into the cushions, never losing contact with her mouth as he plucked and teased at her lips, keeping her fully in the moment. Not content with merely accepting his kiss, she returned it with fervor, taking advantage of his closeness to finally explore his hard physique, trailing her palms and fingers over his firm chest and wide back, tracing the outlines of each muscle in his arms.

He disengaged from the kiss, and she gasped, prompting a chuckle from Nick. His grin slowly dropped as she knelt before him, surprising him as well as herself with her boldness. She hadn't done what she was about to do very often before, but his uninhibited reactions and enjoyment of her combined to give her a confidence she'd never imagined.

She met his gaze then stroked his rigid shaft through his pants. "Is this okay?"

"God, Maggie. Yes." His heartfelt response killed the last of her hesitation and she began working on the fastenings of his pants. He helped by undoing his belt while she unbuttoned and unzipped his jeans. Today his briefs were black and she wondered if he chose them knowing she'd see them. Far from feeling taken for granted, she liked the thought of him dressing to please her. She gave a yank at his waistband and he obligingly lifted his hips so she could get his pants and underwear down to his thighs. She looked in wonder at the perfection of his stiff cock before tentatively kissing the head. His intake of breath gave her renewed confidence and she wrapped her hand around the base of his cock as she licked him slowly around and across the head, marveling at the weight against her tongue, delving into the slit and tasting his tangy essence. She took him into her mouth partway, and the masculine scent and taste of him was surprisingly enticing. Mouthwatering. She sucked hard, and he groaned, grasping her head gently and carefully, shallowly thrusting into her mouth.

Maggie couldn't believe how in tune she felt with Nick. She had never dreamed she would find herself initiating something like this, being with a new man in such an intimate way. She never could have imagined she would be so wanton, feel so sexy and empowered.

The thought tried to intrude that a lasting connection, a relationship with Nick long-term was out of the question. Oh, she would enjoy this while it lasted, no doubt about it. *Really* enjoy it. But she knew that once she left to go back to her mom's, back to being a mom, this would come to a halt. Nick was young and had his life ahead of him, while she was tied to a completely different stage of hers. Somehow she doubted that Nick needed anything from her that he couldn't get from someone with a lot less baggage than her.

She turned away from her negative mental meanderings and continued to work his shaft between her lips and tongue while trailing her fingertips down the deep, muscular vee arrowing from the bottom of his abdominals to the base of his cock. Nick increased the pressure of the fingers tangled in her hair and she smiled inwardly in satisfaction. Her pussy ached with the need for him to fill her, but she was enjoying the feel of his cock on her tongue, stretching her lips.

Still, whatever happened, they would be a lot more comfortable on a bed.

She pulled off him with strong suction, rewarded by a deep groan as he left her lips and his cock smacked back against his lightly haired stomach. "Come on," she invited, rising and holding her hand down to him.

He held her gaze as he rose then pulled up his garments and just fastened the top button.

Maggie was conscious of how disheveled she must look with her lips swollen and her rapid breathing. Instead of bothering her, it made her feel feminine and powerful. "Can we take this upstairs?"

Nick's lips curved in a wicked smile. "After you."

Chapter Nine

Maggie walked up the stairs then led the way down the hall toward the bedroom, feeling Nick's gaze upon her the whole time like a physical touch. She found herself swinging her hips a little more as her breasts tightened with awareness and her pussy clenched in response. Maggie thought back to the years before she and Wade had divorced, after Cass had been born, when he had shared her bed platonically almost every night. She couldn't ever remember experiencing this sort of carnal anticipation.

They entered the bedroom, and she jolted back to reality as Nick picked her up and carried her to the bed, sitting with her across his lap. Maggie snuggled against him and felt a knot inside her loosen, savoring the feel of his strong arms around her as he held her against his solid chest.

"I can't believe this is happening. To me. I just... I haven't ever been this way. I mean, look at me—a grown woman sitting on your lap." She made a move to rise, but he evidently anticipated her action and held her tight.

"You've been alone too long, Maggie," he rumbled under her cheek. He stroked along her back, making her arch into his touch like a cat. "I can feel how much you respond to my touch. Not just in a sexual way, but just holding you."

Maggie took a deep breath and wriggled her bottom against his lap. "I... I've been thinking about you all day. And you're right—not just in that way but also... It just feels good to be held. I miss the affection."

"You hadn't met anyone since you and Wade split then?" Nick queried softly, continuing his slow caresses.

"No one I wanted to bother with. I guess I just wasn't interested," she admitted reluctantly. "I...haven't been with anyone else but you."

His arms tightened around her. "I'm pleased and flattered, Maggie. Thank you. You know"—he ran his hand over her hair—"you might think about dating again after some time goes by and you get your feet back under you. Focusing on being a mom is great, but you're young. You don't want to go through the rest of your life alone."

She didn't, but who would ever want her enough to want to live with her and take on instant fatherhood? Not a very exciting life for most men. *Better to not get my hopes up*, she thought resolutely, a bit saddened but firm. *Even with Nick—he's young and probably wants his own kids, and that's not going to happen here.*

"I don't want to think about that now. I just want to enjoy you while you're here," she murmured against his warm neck, trying to distract both of them by licking and biting down the corded muscles there. "And I think you need a little TLC, too, after your day at work." She gave a nibble followed by a hard suck where his neck met his shoulder, reveling in the solid feel of him against her. For a moment, her emotions welled up as she realized she would most likely be leaving this behind when she had Cassie back home with her. She blinked back tears and shifted so she was astride him, but he wouldn't let her hide her face. He gently lifted her chin and caught her gaze with his as he lowered his lips to hers.

His kiss was everything she craved at that moment, and she threw herself into it completely, pressing her body fully against him, riding his erection with only the material of their clothing between them. Her nipples hardened and peaked against the wall of his chest, and she gave a satisfied little smile as his hands came up to cup and stroke. He groaned as his patience came to an abrupt end and he tore her shirt up over her head rather than unbuttoning it, only pulling his lips from hers long enough to get it off.

He passionately kissed her for an untold length of time before he effortlessly lifted her and flipped her over onto her back on the bed. He unfastened then stripped her pants down her legs, made quick work of her socks and sent them flying along with the remains of her clothing. Nick kept his eyes on hers as he peeled his own shirt off and pushed his jeans down past his knees. Her lips parted when his thick, partially erect cock popped free.

Nick stepped out of his clothing then knelt between her legs and trailed his mouth down from her neck to her breast, giving little nibbles along the way that streaked straight to her aching pussy. After suckling her nipple until she cried out and shifted restlessly, he licked and kissed his way down her stomach, pausing to rim her bellybutton before continuing to her wet pussy, already slick with desire. He hummed with appreciation as he ran his tongue in a broad lick from her entrance to her clit, causing her sex to contract as if trying to draw the passing tongue inside. Nick focused his attention on licking and sucking the nub until she was almost faint with wanting him, squirming and jerking against his firm hold on her hips.

"You're beautiful, Maggie. Love this. I hope you're ready for me, because I'm dying to be inside you again."

Was she supposed to answer that? She could barely think, she was so close to her climax already. "Yes," she breathed and that was apparently enough to satisfy him. The rustle of a wrapper—where had he pulled that from?—then a few moments later he crawled back up over her and nudged her folds with the smooth head of his condom-covered cock. He slowly but steadily filled her, almost too much to take. She was still a bit tender after his previous attentions, but not in a painful way. Just enough to heighten the sensation and make her feel every bit of his possession.

The feel of him pushing his way inside her ratcheted things up fast, too fast, and she unexpectedly hit her peak. As she arched and rippled around him, her hungry passage embracing his length and sucking him farther in, Nick held firm there for a few moments, bracing his bulk above her in a push-up as he watched her climax. Then he began to move, setting a relentless pace with his hips and lower back. He gently lowered his bulk and curled around her, cupping her head, so his lower body rubbed against her swollen clit with each fierce stroke. She felt the tide rise again and they both came together, straining and crying out as the pleasure washed over them with consuming force.

Nick cradled Maggie against him, breathing heavily, waiting for his heartbeat to return to anything approaching normal. The chemistry between them was incredibly intense and he was rocked by how perfect she felt in his arms, how effortlessly they fulfilled each other's needs.

He gently disengaged himself and pressed a kiss to her damp forehead. "I'll be right back." She gave him a faint smile that he returned as he stood then walked to the bathroom.

When Nick came back into the room, instead of finding Maggie lying on the bed as he'd expected, she was unbuttoning and turning her shirt back the right side out, her pants already in place. As she maneuvered her arm into one sleeve of her button-down, he smiled appreciatively at the vision she made all rumpled from sex, though he was disappointed that she hadn't waited for some snuggle time. Evidently even the short couple of minutes he'd taken to clean up had given her too much time to think and the barriers were going back up. She looked up, a blush crawling over her face as her hand rose to hold the edges together before she quickly buttoned up. Her discomfort tugged at his heart.

My heart? That gave him pause. *Already? What am I thinking?*

Maggie had finished buttoning up her shirt and her glance down at his body reminded him that he was stark naked. He wasn't shy, but he knew when it was time to get dressed. He crossed the room and made quick work of putting his clothes on, all without managing to catch Maggie's gaze again. Though she didn't move from the bed, she looked everywhere in the room but at him until he was completely covered.

Really, a guy could get a complex from how quickly she went from being an active partner to wanting him gone.

See? that part of his brain that had tried to warn him earlier chimed in. *Classic booty call.*

C'mon, cut her some slack. Not exactly been a typical few days for her.

"You okay?" he asked, unable to help his frustration at the near repeat performance from last night. Some of what he was feeling must have bled through in his tone of voice, because she looked at him sharply.

"Nick…" Her gaze softened a bit and she held out her hand. He walked over and took it then sat next to her on the side of the bed. "I'm sorry if I seem to be blowing hot and cold. This isn't exactly familiar territory for me, and I have a lot going through my head at the moment."

Guilt washed over him. "Of course you do. I don't mean to add to your stress right now. You have enough going on in your life. I'm a big boy." He smiled wryly. "I don't need special handling. Honest."

"I haven't minded giving you special handling."

That surprised a laugh out of him. "Good. I enjoyed it."

"So did I." Her tone of voice turned wistful and Nick stopped laughing as his stomach dropped. "Look…" She placed her hand on his knee, and the warmth of it burned through his jeans. "I've really loved the time we've spent together."

"Maggie, please don't talk like this is the last we'll see of each other. If you need us to slow down, I have no problem with that."

Maggie jumped to her feet. "This isn't real. This isn't my life. My daughter's not here right now, so it feels like I'm living another person's reality, but this" — she gestured between them—"this can't happen after Cass and I come home. Slowing down implies that there's going to be a progression, but"—she sighed—"I just don't see this going anywhere."

"So that's it?" Nick swallowed down his hurt pride and tried reasoning with her. "I know that you're leaving soon to go be with your daughter..." He trailed off in inquiry.

"Probably day after tomorrow," she confirmed in a soft voice.

Hearing it confirmed was difficult. How had she become entwined in his life so quickly? "I realize that you can't promise anything now. You have a lot to do and help Cassie through this summer. All I'm asking is, after you come back—let's spend some time together." She was already shaking her head, but he forged on. "Who knows? Even if we're just friends to start—"

"Again, that implies you think we might become more, and I just don't think that can happen. We're so different..."

He stood, reminding himself over and over like a mantra that she was grieving and he needed to let her call the shots. Nothing was to be gained from pressing his point right now. Maybe she'd change her mind and reach out to him.

Not likely. It's like the old saying – nice guys finish last.

And he didn't have it in him to be anything other than a gentleman.

Damn it.

To that end, he ignored the common-sense part of his brain and her less-than-welcoming body posture, and dropped a brief kiss on her lips. He didn't trust himself to speak, so he headed out of the bedroom and down the stairs. He stood by the front door until she'd descended, then left the house, waiting to hear the tell-tale snick of the deadbolt engaging behind him before he walked to his car and out of her life.

And if she watched him drive away, he didn't know. He didn't look back.

* * * *

Maggie had never been so eager to get off a plane in her life when the long first flight of her return was over. To go back to economy class after her recent trip in first would have been bad enough, but the whole trip she'd been wishing Nick was there at her side, even crammed into a small seat next to her. She would have willingly sacrificed her personal space for him. Not so for the businessman who'd ended up on her left. He was at least as big as Nick, but not nearly as considerate.

Or sexy.

He'd commandeered the armrest from the start and she'd never had a chance. Then on the window side was an older woman who, bless her, seemed nice...but wouldn't stop talking, even when Maggie had mentioned how she wanted to read/sleep/do the crossword. Four hours of conversation about everything in the woman's life had her wishing desperately that she'd packed ear buds to listen to music or something. No free headphones back here, and she'd passed up the chance to buy them—though if she'd known how unstoppable the woman was going to be, she'd have gladly paid double.

All in all, they weren't the worst row-mates she'd ever had.

But they weren't Nick.

The second flight was a bit easier, not only because it was less than an hour, but also because it was a small jet with a one-two configuration, and she'd lucked into a single seat by herself. That leg of the journey was less about missing Nick and more about psyching herself up for the upcoming horrible conversation with Cassie.

She'd spent a lot of time with only her own thoughts for company by the time she was pulling into the long gravel driveway of her mom's place. She rounded the house and pulled onto the small, paved section in front of the garage, and before she even had the car turned off, Cass was flying out of the house and making a beeline for the driver's side.

"Mom! Mom!"

Maggie exhaled on a half laugh, half sob at the welcome sight of her daughter's dear, excited face. She danced in place next to the driver's door while Maggie turned the car off and grabbed her purse.

Cassie pulled open the door from the outside and was instantly on Maggie in an awkward but very necessary hug. "I didn't think you were ever going to get here! What took you so long?"

"Come on, honey, let your mom get out of the car."

Maggie gave her mom a half smile of gratitude and shared amusement, but it was bittersweet. Sympathy was etched on her mom's face, making her look older than usual.

After finally getting out of the car and giving in to the overwhelming need to stretch, Maggie gave Cassie a proper hug. Then she hugged her mom, who clung tightly for an extra minute to whisper in her ear, "Probably need to do this right away. She's been asking questions I couldn't answer."

Heart sore, Maggie nodded and gave her mom an extra squeeze before letting go. "Thanks, Mom."

She gave Maggie a tentative smile then headed back into the house.

Cass, in one of those intuitive flashes where she demonstrated her growing awareness of the world around her, glanced quickly at the door her grandma disappeared through then focused back on Maggie. "I still don't get why you had to go all the way home and why Grandma's being so weird about it. Every time I try to talk to her about it, she changes the subject to food. What I want for dinner—do I want a snack—should she bake something for dessert."

A fleeting smile crossed Maggie's lips. "That's your grandma for you."

Cass wasn't deterred and continued to study her closely. She was a smart kid and had some kind of sixth sense for when she was being put off.

"Okay, Cass. Let's go in and sit down and I'll answer all your questions." Maggie took Cassie's hand and led the way inside.

The television was on some sort of detective show in the living room, which must be where her mom had gone since she wasn't in the kitchen, so Maggie instead went out to the sunroom. She sat on the couch and Cass sat next to her, not exactly cuddling, but still pretty close.

Maggie took a deep breath then exhaled, trying to decide where to begin. "Remember the night we got here? I got a phone call and after that I was super busy with calls and so forth, then left the next morning?"

Cass nodded. She was looking out of the window, but Maggie could tell that her entire focus was on the conversation. She braced herself to continue, "The phone call was from a police officer, telling me that your dad had been in a car accident."

Cassie whipped her head to face Maggie. "Dad? Was he hurt?"

Oh God. "Yes, honey." She cleared her thickening throat. "They took him to the hospital, and that's why I was flying back. But...on my way home..."

Pressing her lips together, she fought the emotions but moisture welled up in her eyes. "I don't know how to tell you this." Somehow needing to get it out before the tears overflowed, she also looked outside and forced herself to go on quietly, "Your dad died that morning."

There was an immediate intake of breath but not another sound or movement from Cass for several long moments. Her weight seemed to increase its pressure along Maggie's side where they touched. Maggie turned toward Cassie again, and she could tell from the lost and overwhelmingly painful expression on Cassie's crumpling face that the words and their meaning had definitely registered—that Cass knew what it meant.

"What?" The rhetorical question was barely audible, but the next sentence was crystal clear. "Dad... No. Daddy. He can't be dead. He's not"—Cass made a windmill gesture that turned into a fist—"not...old. No, no...*nooooo*..." This last was not quite a word, more of a wail as her mouth dropped open and the tears began to fall for both of them. Maggie gathered Cass against her, halfway on her lap as Cass' sobs became increasingly loud and hysterical.

At some point her mom had joined them and wrapped them both in her embrace. They all rocked together as they fought to get over that first blinding shock of Cassie hearing and processing the news.

There would be more questions later, Maggie was sure—so much grief and anger and sadness to come. But the initial, painful blow had landed and Maggie let herself cry alongside her daughter—for her, with her. It was no less than Wade deserved. The man had been a devoted and loving father, and Maggie's partner and best friend for so many years. It still didn't seem real that she would never see him again, that Cass would have to go through all of the milestones to come in her life without Wade being there.

Even as she wept into her daughter's hair, Maggie pressed her lips together in determination. She was going to have to be both parents from now on, the only parent, and concentrate all of her focus on Cassie.

All they had was each other now.

Chapter Ten

The quiet of the house was deafening, and Maggie sighed just to hear something. The second day of the school year. She'd known it was going to be hard to lose Cassie's constant presence—she always got so used to it over the summer break. But this year it was even harder and more poignant.

So she'd sent Cass off to school on the bus this morning, then hadn't done much of anything. After Maggie had informed Cassie's new teacher in a quiet aside about Wade's death at the school supply drop-off night last week, a conference had been set up a couple of days ago that included Maggie, Cassie's teachers, the school counselor and principal. They would all keep a close eye on Cassie to make sure she was handling things okay as she transitioned back to school while continuing to deal with her grief. Maggie had been a bit surprised but gratified to learn that the counselor led a monthly lunch meeting with kids dealing with issues in their home life, including divorce and death. She'd had no idea, and wondered to the assembled group whether she should have informed the school about the divorce the prior school year. They'd assured Maggie that they hadn't noticed it affecting Cass, and indeed, the impression had been that they were still a couple since they often showed up for school events as a trio.

Excited to be back with her friends, Cassie had actually spent that last few weeks looking forward to the first day of school. So had Maggie, in a way, but for a very different reason. With Cass practically glued to her side all summer, she hadn't been able to do much of anything about Wade's apartment. It was now on a month-to-month lease, and she really needed to get it cleaned out, but that was not something she wanted Cassie around for. As it was, the few times she'd gone over there while Cassie had spent time at Sam's, she'd come home with mementos and things she wanted to keep, and it always set Cassie off to see them. Sometimes tears, sometimes just withdrawal. So she wanted to minimize the exposure.

She'd spent a good part of yesterday sorting and packing things there and really should be back at it today, but she needed a break—more just from the constant decision-making about what should stay, go and be donated.

Enough thinking. That's all you do anymore, Maggie Jean.

Speaking of which, she should really start sorting through Cassie's clothes and start culling the too-small stuff, but she wasn't in the mood. It might be time to dust off her résumé and start looking for a job, but she still wanted to be home when Cassie was, and not many jobs offered school-hour and holiday flexibility. Maybe something online, though...

Diverted by that thought, she made herself a fresh cup of coffee, then went into the office and sat down in front of the computer. She turned it on to boot it up. As it was going through start-up, she idly looked over the stacks of papers by the inboxes. She didn't think all the paperwork for Wade would ever end.

Her gaze sharpened on a business card.

Nick…

The mere sight of the card brought back the seductive memory of that crazy time early this summer, when she'd let her libido rule her brain. She'd spent a couple of months trying her best to forget those nights. And she'd been partially successful, especially during the days in which she'd had Cassie's heartbroken reaction to losing her father to deal with, as well as all the myriad tasks and frustrations which came with dealing with the death of a family member.

She'd relegated Nick to a memory of a kind of mental breakdown, a doomed one-nighter — well, technically a two-nighter — with a kid in his twenties that couldn't have possibly gone anywhere. She'd needed to grow up and focus on Cassie, not be selfish.

But Nick wasn't easily forgotten. Sitting here now, Maggie could still recall very clearly the taste of Nick's kisses, the solid weight of him, the trust-inducing way he'd cared for her. She stared at the card then reached out and picked it up. Turning it over, she spotted his personal email address written under his phone numbers.

Maggie glanced at the computer then back at the card.

What are the chances he still even remembers you?

Well, he probably remembered her. But that didn't necessarily mean he'd want to hear from her, especially after all this time. He could be dating someone. For all she knew, he had been when they'd gotten together. Or he could have just moved on and wouldn't find her as attractive as when they'd been in the first rush of passion they'd shared.

If it had just been a physical attraction, it would be easy to toss the card and move on with her life. But Maggie still had a huge part of her that still missed Nick's presence. That part of her wasn't pulling any punches right now, goading her to give in and call him. Hear that deep voice saying her name.

She toyed with the card a bit longer, then set it down and walked away.

* * * *

A grand total of frustrating three hours later, she was back in the office looking down at the card again. She was too spooked to call and possibly hear dismissal in his voice, or worse, that he didn't even remember her. After all, they'd only spent a handful of hours together, a long time ago. So instead, she decided to send him an email. She'd kept it brief, only a few sentences asking how he'd been and telling him she'd been fine, but it had taken her the better part of an hour to compose.

Hi Nick,

I hope you had a great summer and this finds you well. Sorry it's taken me so long to get in touch. It was a very difficult and busy summer, but things are going okay now. I've been thinking of you recently and wanted to let you know how much I appreciate all you did for me during that dark time earlier this year. You certainly went above and beyond, and I'm very grateful. I'd love to hear from you when you have a chance.

Take care,
Maggie

To her shock and secret delight, he had replied almost immediately, and his warmth and personality rang through his missive, making her miss him even more.

Hi Maggie!
So great to hear from you! I've been thinking about you, too. Both you and Cass. I'm sure it's been extremely hard, but you're a very strong woman, and I know that you've been a rock for your daughter. I wish I could have been there to support you, and please know that the offer is open any time you need someone to lean on.
I'd love to hear your voice. Call me sometime. Anytime.
Hugs,
Nick

It was as though the conflicted part of her began to dissolve at his words. Simple words on a screen, but they reached in and touched her heart.

The self-loathing she'd felt after their couple of nights together had been hard to deal with, but she'd finally seen their brief affair for what it was—an affirmation of life. What had been hardest about it was how disloyal she'd felt to Wade, scant hours after his death, to have experienced elsewhere the passion she'd never felt with him—what he'd eventually gone to look for elsewhere.

She finally began to accept how upset his infidelity had made her, how much it had hurt her. Maggie had tried so hard to keep things peaceful for Cassie's sake, she hadn't given in to her honest right to her anger. And Wade had only benefitted from her tacit acceptance of his straying, getting off scot-free, which made her angry at his memory—creating a whole new level of guilt.

So many 'what ifs' had gone through her head, and the grief and guilt and exhaustion had all combined to make her do what she'd feared to be the stupidest thing she'd ever done—ruthlessly pushing a man like Nick out of her life. A man who was everything she'd never known she wanted, and who had treated her like some precious gift without thought for himself.

Now, Maggie had an opening for a second chance.

She smiled and hit reply.

Chapter Eleven

Maggie checked her inbox with more eagerness than she should have felt, hoping for a message, however impersonal, from Nick. Disappointment rang through her—nothing.

Since those first couple of stilted emails, they'd gotten into the habit of sharing their days and thoughts with one another via that medium and the occasional IM. Every few emails, he'd close with, "Call me sometime," but not once in the past couple of months had she heard his voice. She hadn't yet had the nerve to pick up the phone.

"Hey, Mom. Can I check my inbox too?"

Cassie was still very excited about having her very own email address. She corresponded mainly with Maggie's mom and a couple of cousins, as well as a few school friends she saw every day anyway. "Sure, sweetie, let me switch over."

"I can do it!"

"Okay, okay, go ahead." Maggie slid out of the chair and ceded it to her daughter. She headed to the kitchen and heard a ping from the computer.

"Who's Nick?" Cassie called.

Maggie's heart almost stopped in her chest, and she hurried back to the computer. An IM box had popped up in the lower corner.

Nick: R U there?

Maggie nudged her daughter, who reluctantly stood up. "He's a friend of mine, sweetie."

Maggie: I'm here. Day off?
Nick: On nights.

"Like a boyfriend type of friend?" her daughter asked guilelessly. Maggie froze and turned her full attention to Cassie. She heard another ping, but ignored it for now.

"No," she answered slowly. "But...what would you think about that if he was?" She held her breath as she waited for Cassie's answer, searching for any sign of upset.

Cassie shrugged. "That would be kind of cool. Caylyn's mom has a boyfriend, and he takes her shopping and to the movies and stuff. And they went camping."

Maggie's eyebrows rose. "You want to go camping?" She shook her head, laughing a bit inwardly at being so easily distracted by minutiae. She also recognized her inner amusement was partially relief at Cassie's seeming acceptance. "So it would be okay with you if I went out with Nick sometime?" she sought to clarify.

"Sure, Mom." Cassie gave her a look that made her seem years older. "You sometimes seem kinda lonely. I know Dad's not coming back, and I don't want you to be alone forever." Tears welled up in Cassie's eyes and Maggie's vision blurred as well. They hugged for a long time, and Maggie finally processed the persistent ping of another couple of IM's piling up.

Wiping her daughter's face, she instructed, "Go find a tissue. You're leaking all over me." Cassie made a face, and Maggie watched lovingly as she ran from the room, leaving her alone to wipe her own tears.

Turning back to the computer, she read the IM's that had piled up.

Nick: Have a couple of days off starting tomorrow.
Nick: Maybe we could do something?

Then, a couple of minutes later —

Nick: Sorry, my mistake. I understand. Bye, Maggie.

His status now showed offline.

Oh crap. Now he thought she hadn't answered him on purpose. Anxiety seized her, and she opened a new email message, then stopped.

Maggie ran upstairs to her bedroom and pulled open the drawer of her bedside table, taking out the card with Nick's numbers on it. She'd taken it up to her bedroom to keep things private between them, knowing that Cass was pretty sharp and since she used the office for the computer pretty often, eventually if it was down there, she would notice it and ask about it.

Figuring that if Nick had been on the computer he was at home, she started with his home number, becoming more and more frustrated and agitated as she got no answer. When the messaging picked up, she wasn't prepared, and she hung up.

Determined to fix his perception that she was ignoring him or upset, she quickly scanned the second phone number and dialed his cell. It rang and rang, and just as she despaired of getting through to him, he answered, his voice sounding thick and gruff.

"Hello?"

"Nick?"

"Maggie?" He cleared his throat. "Hi. Sorry, I had just gone to bed."

Immediately, her mind flashed to the vision of his naked form in her bed. She just barely restrained herself from asking what he was wearing...or not.

"I'm sorry. I didn't mean to wake you."

"Mmm—" Then he groaned. Logically, she knew he was probably just stretching, but the sounds shot straight to her overwrought libido. "Okay, so, how are you?"

"Doing good. Better. I had a great conversation with Cassie this morning. That's why I went AWOL on our IM like that, not because I didn't want to answer or anything. She just...caught me off guard by starting a discussion that was probably past due just then."

"What about?" His sleepy, gravelly tone was sinful.

"About whether you were my boyfriend and if that would be okay if you were." Silence from the other end. Silence she had to fill. "So, I mean...maybe you're dating someone else by now, and I wouldn't blame you if you were, but— If you were free and wanted to... I mean—"

"Maggie," he interrupted, all traces of tiredness gone from his voice. "What are you doing right now?"

"Now?" It came out almost a squeak. "Um, nothing. Not really."

"You're at home?"

"Yes, why — ?" she started to ask and he cut her off again.

"I'm coming over. This is a conversation I really want to have in person. Okay?" He didn't wait for an answer. "I'll be there in fifteen." He hung up.

She blinked at her phone for a full minute before it hit her.

Nick.

Was coming here.

Now.

"Oh my God." Maggie rushed to the bathroom and grimaced at the sight of herself in the mirror. She ran a brush through her hair viciously and stepped out of her mules, kicking them toward the closet. "Clothes, clothes," she muttered to herself, frantically perusing her closet as she undressed, mentally discarding choice after choice.

"Oh hell." She finally just pulled on a newish pair of jeans and a long-sleeved knit top. No bra. That made her smile, remembering the plane ride.

Back in the bathroom, she washed her face and flossed and brushed her teeth, then looked around. Deciding not to worry about the state of the bedroom — after all, Cassie was home — she flew downstairs to start picking up the living room.

"Cassie!" she yelled, and soon her daughter skidded around the corner.

"What? What'd I do?"

Maggie laughed, feeling slightly giddy. "Nothing, hon. Here, help me pick up in here. Hurry!"

"But Mom, I was — "

Maggie continued to grab stuff. "No buts. You want me to have a boyfriend or not? 'Cause he's on his way over right now."

"Oh. Oh!" Comprehension hit, and Cassie grabbed all the stuff in Maggie's arms and sped across the room to throw it in a closet. "Go put some makeup on."

"What?" Maggie went still and stared at Cassie. "You think I need makeup?"

The doorbell rang and they looked at the door then back at each other. "I'll get it," Cassie decided.

Maggie hovered in the living room as Cassie confidently crossed to the door. "Who is it?" she called in a sing-songy voice then grinned at her mom.

"It's Nick, a friend of your mom's." The sound of his voice in person for the first time in months, even muffled by the door, sent shivers through Maggie, which only multiplied as Cassie opened the door to reveal Nick himself.

Her memory hadn't done him justice. He looked bigger and more muscular than she remembered, which she could easily see since he didn't have a coat on…

"Oh, you must be freezing, come in," Maggie invited hastily. He stepped in and threw a smoldering look at her before looking down at Cassie who was unabashedly observing their guest.

"Hi, you must be Cassie." He offered his hand.

"And you must be Nick, the *boyfriend*."

That little imp.

Nick only smiled at the precocious taunt. "It's nice to finally meet you. I'm looking forward to getting to know you." He looked down at the cat twining between his legs.

"That's Champ. He must like you."

"Cass, can you please excuse us for a little while?"

Cass groaned theatrically, but picked up Champ and headed for the stairs. "Come on, Champy, we can't hear the grown-up talk."

The two adults watched her disappear upstairs then turned to each other. As their gazes locked, Maggie couldn't restrain herself any longer, and she quickly crossed to walk straight into his welcoming arms.

Nick hugged her so tightly against his chest she was reduced to shallow breaths. "I thought you'd never call," he confessed gruffly.

"Oh, Nick. I wanted to, for the longest time. I just didn't know how to—put myself out there, I guess. Especially after how I treated you that last night."

He frowned down at her. "Haven't we taken care of all that since we've been 'talking' these last couple of months? Haven't we become friends?"

Yes, but I want more.

"Yes. We're friends. But it's different in person."

"Better," he countered confidently.

"Better," she agreed and took a deep breath. "Nick—" Maggie paused to gather her thoughts. "I'm so glad to see you. I don't ever want to be apart like that again."

She waited for his reaction to her statement, which was tantamount to her asking to be together—really together, like a couple.

"I don't ever want to be apart—period."

His answer was all she had hoped for and more. She could see the desire for her in his eyes and felt it in the way he held her, and thanked God she had finally broken the ice.

Or maybe she should thank Cassie. Speaking of which… "Go to your room!"

A giggle from the stairs and thumping feet confirmed her suspicions.

"I guess you're officially my boyfriend now. Cassie will be thrilled."

Nick grinned. "As long as you're thrilled too, that makes it unanimous."

"I am," she agreed, snuggling closer to him as they rocked together. "Oh, and Nick?"

"Hmm?"

"How do you feel about camping?"

* * * *

The timing couldn't have been better, since thankfully Nick wasn't working the next couple of days. He was tired but the adrenaline shot that had raced through him at the sound of Maggie's voice — make that a double shot when she'd said she was willing to try — had gone a long way toward sustaining him. They'd spent the rest of the evening together, with Nick and Cassie getting to know each other, and Maggie and Nick relearning each other.

He'd gotten to the point where he figured it was a lost cause, that Maggie wasn't ever going to reach out to him. He probably would have contacted her eventually, but then again, maybe not. She'd been pretty clear when she'd told him goodbye that she had strong reasons for doing so, and it wouldn't have been his place to contradict the validity of her feelings.

Now he was downstairs while Maggie tucked a wound-up but tired Cassie into bed. At a loss for something to do, he picked up the plates and glasses on the coffee table, rinsed them in the kitchen and put them in the dishwasher. He walked around and checked the doors and windows, glad to see that everything was closed up tight. Though, when he left he'd need to make sure she locked up behind him.

He didn't want to leave.

But he also didn't want to blow this second chance.

Maggie came around the corner from the direction of the stairs and smiled at him, as she'd been doing frequently all evening. It was bit of a startling contrast to his memories of her, but he definitely liked it.

"You must be really tired."

"Past tired, actually, but it's okay. I'm having a good time," he answered truthfully, not wanting the evening to end.

Maggie joined him on the couch, and the way she slotted herself in next to him as he put his arm around her was so natural it sent his heart soaring.

She gave a contented sigh. "Me too, but I'm going to need to call it a night pretty soon. School day tomorrow, so I have to be up with Cass."

Disappointment had him closing his eyes for a moment. "I should let you get to bed then."

"Okay." She rose and he followed suit. They walked around the couch but when he headed to the front door, she went in the other direction toward the stairs.

"I know you want to get to bed, but you need to lock the front door."

"You cops." She shook her head, though a smile teased at the corners of her mouth. "I figured you would have already checked it by now."

Nick frowned slightly. "I did," he admitted, "but you need to lock up…after…I leave…" He trailed off as Maggie's smile grew until she was sporting a full-on, wicked grin.

"Who says you need to leave?" She angled herself toward the stairs, but maintained eye contact with him and held out her hand.

His heart started thudding in his chest as her words and actions registered. "What about Cassie?"

"I say we sleep now—you're exhausted, don't lie—and after I get her off to school in the morning, we can...catch up." Maggie lost a bit of her bravado and blushed for the first time.

Hating to see even a hint of uncertainty in her eyes, Nick quickly crossed to her and gathered her in his embrace. He pressed a gentle kiss to her lips then held her head between his hands. "I would love to...catch up with you."

She turned even redder but met his gaze without hesitation. "That's... I'm glad."

Nick couldn't resist one more kiss before he began to walk with her upstairs. Tonight he would have Maggie back in his arms, and tomorrow...

Tomorrow would be the start of the rest of their lives.

He couldn't wait.

SPRING TRAINING

Dedication

With love to my real life inspirations:

Teresa, who showed courage, humor, and energy in raising her twins from such a young age. You did great, little mama. Hope you like my Alex and Em.

And Theresa, the biggest baseball fan I know, with a four-pack of boys and a donated kidney — endlessly positive and energetic. I'm truly blessed to have you for a sister-in-law.

Prologue

"Heads up, it's a bunt! He's putting it down!" Teri screamed, cupping her hands around her mouth. The infielders were already reading the stance of the batter and moving forward in anticipation.

Sure enough, the batter skillfully laid a soft bunt down the third base line and took off for first, and with bases loaded, everyone was running.

Teri jumped to her feet. "Home, force at home!" she yelled as if she could be heard over the roar of the crowd. Her eyes were glued to the third baseman.

He charged the ball, snagging it on the run then deftly flipping it to the catcher for the out at home.

"Turn two, turn two!"

The catcher heaved the ball to first, just past the head of the batter, and Teri watched, heart in her throat, for the call from the umpire.

Before he'd even finished his "Out!" signaling the successful double play, she was in the air with a whoop, looking automatically to the tall, rangy third baseman, who was pointing straight at her with a crooked grin. She blew him a kiss, and the handsome ballplayer winked back before running to join his teammates celebrating their victory with a huge dogpile on the pitcher's mound. It was early in the season yet, but a return trip to the College World Series in Omaha was looking more and more likely.

Fingers crossed.

Her heart pounding with adrenaline, and still feeling giddy from being on the receiving end of that beautiful smile, Teri turned a bit sheepishly to the tall, equally handsome man standing and clapping next to her on the bleachers. He was looking down at her with a familiar combination of amusement and embarrassment. As soon as their eyes met, she threw her arms around his middle in an apologetic hug.

"Do I know you?" he mocked.

Teri smiled against his shirt. "Know me and love me."

"You love *him* more." He patted her on the head.

It was a frequent complaint, without heat, and one she always had an answer for. "I love you both the same, just differently."

"Yeah, right." Alex gave her one last squeeze before setting her aside. "I'm going down. You coming?" He rolled his eyes dramatically. "What am I saying? Of course you're coming. Stick close to me—it's a mob scene down there."

Teri grinned as her protective 'older' son grabbed her hand and used his height to his advantage in shouldering his way through the masses toward the dugout of the celebrating players, tugging her along in his wake. They successfully navigated the stadium steps then worked their way along the walkway until they could get down to field level.

One body separated itself from the team and was suddenly thumping against them, enveloping them both in a hard, sweaty embrace.

"Get off me, fucker, you're gross."

"Alex! Watch your mouth."

"Sorry, Mom, but he *is* gross."

"That's *not* the word I meant, and you know it." She turned to her youngest son, Emery—youngest by a whole five minutes—and reached up to take his face in her hands. "Great play at the end, Em. Good hustle. They never would've gotten the batter in time if it'd been anyone else."

Emery flushed with pleasure at the compliment, even as he contradicted, "Jeez, Ma, you're not biased or anything. That's a play any good third baseman should've made."

"Be that way. I know you're awesome." She stretched on tiptoes to kiss his cheek. "You coming with us to grab a bite after you clean up?" It was a rhetorical question, of course. Emery was a growing boy and never missed a chance to eat, especially after a game *and* when Teri was paying. She was all about giving her boys choices, though, even obvious ones.

"Excuse me, Emery Sandusky?"

The family turned as one toward the unfamiliar voice.

"Yeah, I'm Emery." Em froze when he saw who was speaking.

Teri's smile glued itself to her lips and she carefully watched Em. He swallowed and glanced at his head coach, who was standing slightly behind the stranger.

"Bill Patterson." The man offered his hand to Em, who thankfully had the presence of mind to accept it for a shake. "Your coach and I have been talking. Do you have a minute?"

Teri's breath caught— *Oh my God, it is a scout*—and she practically shoved Em toward the two men. "You go, hon. We'll be at Culver's. On second thought, we're driving through. I'll get you the usual. See you at home. C'mon, Alex." She pulled on his arm frantically and aimed him toward the car.

"What's the hurry? Didn't you want to hear what he had to say?" Alex reluctantly allowed her to lead him back up to the walkway out of the college stadium.

Teri didn't answer right away, her mind churning over the possibility of Emery getting his break into professional ball. There was no doubt in her mind he had the talent. She'd been watching every level of baseball for years and knew her son had 'it'—that quality from which stars were made. Her concern was more for his level of commitment and focus. All the knowledge of the game and physical talent in the world couldn't make up for a lack of drive and the immature antics she knew him to be capable of.

She sighed and reminded herself Emery was still a kid, a pretty typical twenty-one-year-old. Teri had just never been able to rein him in all the way, and as a result, she and his more level-headed twin brother were always bailing him out of one bad scrape after another. Oh, nothing major... *Yet,* she added cynically. But he was still a worry to her in a way Alex had never been.

It was one of the rare moments Teri regretted not having anything to do with their biological dad. Maybe having a father-figure around would have been what Em needed. Even as the thought occurred to her, she was shaking her head, negating it. The twins had been the result of her first, and only, sexual escapade in college, with an older student who, unbeknownst to her, had already fathered a kid by another girl.

When she'd turned up pregnant, he'd shown his true colors and had not been exactly supportive. His parents had joined forces with hers, though, and the young couple had acceded to their wishes and tried a brief, disastrous marriage soon after the boys were born. He'd gone on to cheat on her when the twins were toddlers, and that had been that.

She and the boys had done well by each other, and as they grew, the differences in the two became more evident. Alex was quieter and more studious, while Emery was the life of the party and had a tendency to struggle in school, mostly from lack of interest. He and Alex had started out about as identical as could be, but now they looked more like brothers than twins, which suited them just fine. Alex was more slender, with a runner's form, while Emery hit the weights and was much broader and more muscular. Alex alone needed glasses, although he usually wore contacts. Emery wore his dark brown hair longer than his brother, in a sort of rebellious, shapeless shag that stuck out from under his ball cap.

Teri smiled up at her more clean-cut son and looped her arm through his, finally responding, "You know I'd love to be a fly on the wall, but Emery doesn't need his mom hovering over him for this. His coach is there with him. He'll do fine." She hoped. "I'm sure we'll hear all the details a hundred times. Let's go pick up some dinner—you know your brother's going to be starved."

Please let him get his shot…and not screw it up.

Chapter One

Six weeks later

Aaron rolled his shoulder gingerly then scowled down at the oily rag in his hand. Bad enough that he wasn't able to be at his real home, working out with his team for spring training, but now Coach had talked him into babysitting duty for the new young phenom he'd brought into the organization. A phenom that was currently AWOL. Not exactly an auspicious start.

His cell phone rang just as he was getting into a good rhythm. "Damn it. Great timing, Deke." After looking around fruitlessly for a sec, he finally just wiped his oily hands down his jeans. They were old anyway.

When he finally picked the phone up, he had to smile at the contact photo of his friend getting knocked ass over teakettle during a play at home. "Hey, man," he answered.

"Hank! Wut up?" Deke's low drawl was as thick and strong as Deke himself.

"Not much." He stood and walked over to the sliding door to the balcony, staring out at the forested greenbelt behind the condo complex. He'd closed the door earlier because some random neighbor somewhere had been smoking. "Just doing some chores. Day off." He slid the door open and sniffed to make sure the air was unpolluted before stepping out. One thing he couldn't stand was the smell of smoke. Probably came from growing up with a dad who'd constantly smoked in the house. He'd had enough second-hand carcinogens in his lifetime.

"So how long ya gonna be down on the farm makin' hay?"

Aaron had to chuckle at the creative reference to his current position with one of their minor league teams — or 'farm teams'. Deke might fool those who didn't know him into thinking he was some dumb hick, but he was sharp and had a wicked quick sense of humor. "Probably until my country accent's as thick as yours, boy." He sat on the chaise longue and swung his legs up onto the seat.

"Hain't never gonna happen. This here took decades to perfect." After a brief laugh, Deke added in a more serious tone, "You ain't worried 'bout the long run, are ya? The docs haven't said anything else?"

"Nothing new." Aaron shrugged reflexively then winced. He kept forgetting. "It'll just take time and determination." *And luck.*

"And you got those in spades, or your name ain't Hank Aaron Reynolds, son."

"Amen, brother."

"How's the wet nursin' going?"

"Typical." Aaron wasn't a gossip, but this was Deke, and he knew that whatever he said wouldn't go anywhere. Well, maybe with the exception of his wife,

Julia, but she was similar to Deke in that she was trustworthy. They had both proven it many times before, especially during this time in Aaron's career. Everyone knew that Aaron and Deke were best friends, so Deke and Julia got asked questions about him a lot but never volunteered anything.

"So he's basically young and cocky and full of himself?"

"Sort of. Yeah, on the face of it. Seems to have decent manners, though, so it might not be too bad. That said, he didn't come home last night."

Deke gave a snort. "What, already? He's only been there a day, right?"

"Yep." He sighed. Aaron had seen Emery Sandusky's footage with the rest of the coaching staff, and he was a heck of a ballplayer. He played third base like he'd been born for it, plus he was a natural hitter. But it hadn't taken much digging to find out he was a partier, so Coach had asked Aaron to open up his condo to the young man, to try to insulate him as best he could and be a steadying influence.

Even so, Emery'd disappeared his first night in town with some of the other younger players.

Deke grunted disgustedly and Aaron continued, "I didn't expect to have to lay down the law about curfew and house rules before the kid even unpacked. I suppose I'll have to have a chat with him today. If he ever comes home," he added, looking at the clock. They had a day off today but would be expected to hit it hard starting tomorrow. "I was going to take him over to the field and show him around so he knows what to expect when he walks in tomorrow."

"That's nice of ya, Dad."

"Shove it," Aaron shot back without any heat. "Speaking of dads, how's Julia coming along? She got that baby baked yet?"

"Still cookin', Uncle Hank," Deke answered proudly. After a couple of years of effort, complicated by the team's travelling schedule, Deke and Julia had finally managed to get the deed done. His best friend couldn't wait to be a daddy. "You'd best heal up and come on back, 'cause if you ain't here when this baby comes, Julia will never forgive ya."

Aaron smirked. "Yeah, I'm sure it's Julia that won't be happy."

Deke laughed his cheerful, deep chuckle. "That's all I'm coppin' to. We get to take a gander at it tomorrow, maybe find out if it's a boy or girl if he don't have his legs crossed."

"Or *her* legs," Aaron pointed out.

"I'll be glad when we find out, man. I hate callin' the baby 'it' and every fuckin' time I say one or t'other someone corrects me."

Aaron laughed. "Yeah, that'll come in handy."

"I'd best be goin'. Don't be a stranger, 'kay?"

"Yeah, man. I'll touch base in a couple days."

"You do that. See ya."

Aaron said goodbye and hung up then stretched. He really didn't have much to do today. He'd already gone to the store to stock up on food for the week, done some light cleaning and caught up on emails. Maybe he'd go for a jog after he put a bit more time into the glove he was breaking in.

He went back inside and settled into the soothing rhythm of working oil into leather. He'd been at it for about ten minutes when he heard the sound of a key in the lock. He looked up from the glove as the front door of the condo opened. His new charge came through the door, looking a bit worse for the wear, slamming the door behind him in his haste.

Here we go.

Having great skills at ball didn't always translate into life skills, and this guy was, as Deke had so succinctly put, a typical, cocky young guy. Aaron sighed. When he'd offered to help out his old coach while doing rehab, he'd figured that would mean running outfielders' drills and encouraging players during training. He hadn't thought he'd be stuck mentoring a party boy one-on-one. But the kid was promising enough to McCauley that he had a vested interest in keeping him on the straight and narrow. He tried to remember that and put a welcoming smile on his face.

"Hey, Aaron, how's it going?" Emery greeted him.

At least he was somewhat polite. His parents had evidently taught him some manners, though a bit more discipline when he was younger might have gone a long way toward curbing his antics. He'd only been here for about a day, and he was already staying out all night—drinking, from the looks of him. Emery plopped down in the chair next to him at the table. *And the smell of him.* Time would tell whether it was the start of a bad habit, or just an understandable one-time celebration of his new circumstances.

"Hi, Emery. Pretty good." He added more oil to his rag then began spreading it on the glove he was conditioning. "Have fun last night?" Inwardly he winced at hearing his father's disapproving and sarcastic voice coming out of his mouth.

Thankfully, his tone went right over Emery's bed-head. "Oh yeah. There are some guys I know from college ball, so they showed me around. Met a chick.

You know…" Emery shrugged and slouched back into the chair.

Aaron did know, though he'd usually avoided the bleacher babes that buzzed around ballplayers. He gave one head tilt in response, barely keeping from rolling his eyes. He was less than ten years older than Emery, but he felt ancient next to his youthful obliviousness.

"Oh!" Emery sat up straight. "Crap. What time is it? I'd better get cleaned up."

Aaron frowned. "It's around noon. What's up?"

Emery stood, a slow, genuine grin softening his face. "I hope you don't mind, but my number one fan is driving down today and I told her she could stay here while she's in town."

Jesus. The kid had a girlfriend coming to stay and he'd just gotten back from getting laid last night?

Emery's smile slowly dropped when Aaron didn't respond right away. "That's not a problem, is it?"

"No, man. Whatever. *Mi casa es su casa.*" He nodded at Emery, hiding his disgust. He never could understand cheaters. Why commit to someone then fuck around? He nodded to Emery's less than stellar appearance. "You might want to clean up, though."

"Yeah, good idea. She'd freak if she saw me like this at this time of day." Instead of going to his still unpacked room, though, Emery first headed to the kitchen.

Aaron was still shaking his head when a knock came at the door. Well, more of a pounding, really, that had him jumping up to answer just to get it to stop.

Jesus. That better not be the cops or an angry husband or something.

Teri's hands and arms were full of the reusable grocery bags she'd hauled up to Emery's new apartment. Unable to knock, she kicked the door three times hard. No answer. And she'd just talked to him ten minutes ago. "C'mon, Em," she muttered, pulling her foot back for another 'knock'.

Instead of resistance, her foot met air as the door opened. Thrown off balance, she took a desperate step forward, trying to regain her balance.

"Whoa."

She was caught firmly by the elbow and steadied by a large, strong grip.

"You must be 'the number one fan'," the unfamiliar voice added with a touch of sarcasm.

You must be Aaron, the apparently grumpy roommate.

Finally stable, she looked up, expecting to see a young man around her sons' age.

Boy, was she wrong. In a good way.

Suddenly hyperaware of the hand still grasping her arm, she fought for composure. Her over-stimulated primary erogenous zone—her brain—was having a field day as the man in front of her tripped every trigger she possessed at once.

Tall, muscular and athletic? Check.

Tawny, sun-kissed skin and blond hair? Uh-huh.

Deep celadon green eyes with little laugh lines at the edges? Nice touch.

She inhaled deeply. Gads, he even smelled heavenly. Male, spicy and a little bit like...glove oil?

Rowr.

The squint lines were promising. Maybe—hopefully—he wasn't nearly as young as she'd expected. Or maybe they were just from playing ball in the sun for so many years and she was a total perv. She glanced down at the elbow he still held.

"Oh, damn, sorry about that." He removed the oily rag he was holding in the hand supporting her, swiping at her skin ineffectually with his thumb. At least, it was ineffective at removing the grease. It was proving pretty effective at something else though…

Her eyes narrowed as something about his face gave her a prod of recognition.

Aaron? Hmm…

Trying to place him, and realizing she hadn't yet said a word, she finally responded, "No problem." She was proud of how normal her voice sounded.

Get a grip, Sandusky. You sooo need a man if you're lusting after your son's roommate.

Gratefully seizing upon the grounding effect of the thought of her son, she continued, "You must be Aaron. Is Emery here?"

"Yes." He backed in a bit reluctantly. "C'mon in, he just rolled in. I'll try to catch him before he gets in the shower."

Teri frowned, distracted from her hormonal mental wanderings. "Just rolled in? You mean, from being out last night?" *Oh, great.*

Aaron shifted, looking uncomfortable, but before he could answer, Em strolled into the living room. "Ma, hey!"

"Ma?" Aaron echoed incredulously, going still.

Emery crossed the room in a couple of big strides and gave her a hug. *Whoa.* Almost overcome with the stench as his unbound hair fell against her face, she reared back, pushing him away and gaping at him.

"Emery! Have you been smoking?" She took another careful sniff, and the sharp tang of alcohol was unmistakable. She'd unfortunately learned over the years that his body chemistry processed alcohol in a very recognizable manner through his pores. Her heart clenched. "You reek of alcohol," she stated flatly, staring him down.

"What?" Em shot back, but had the grace to flush as he tried to take a sniff of himself, evidently so used to it he couldn't smell it anymore. "It was just a little getting to know the team thing last night." He fiddled with the belt loops of his jeans as he avoided eye contact.

Disappointment clamored and Teri tried to swallow it down. Only one day, and he was already partying. With one last look at her son's averted face, she turned toward the kitchen. "Go take a shower. We'll talk when you get out." She was already dreading the conversation, one she could predict almost down to the exact words. The excuses, the defensiveness, the promises.

Damn it, Em. When are you going to grow up?

She'd had reservations about his quitting college to take this shot at pro ball, but he'd vowed to take it seriously. Pressing her lips together to try to keep from swearing out loud—or, worse, tearing up—she entered the small kitchen, set down the bags then began to put away the perishables she'd impulsively bought for Em at the natural foods store she'd spotted on the way into town. His favorite yoghurt, orange-peach-mango juice, hummus and red peppers—the only raw vegetable she didn't have to fight to make him eat. The contents of the fridge surprised her a bit—she'd expected to see only beer, pop and ketchup. Instead, she had to work to make room for the peppers in the crisper drawer amongst an assortment of other veggies.

She sensed movement behind her as she finished, and straightened to find Aaron putting away the non-perishables from one of the other sacks in the small pantry. He turned away quickly as she stood, gaze sliding away from the vicinity of her backside. She raised a mental eyebrow. He was checking out her ass? She snorted. Now *there* was something that didn't happen every day. If she'd known, she might've put on some makeup and worn something besides loose yoga pants and a T-shirt. But comfort was way more important to her than trying to compete with the pretty, young things who could always be found hanging around the teams. Especially while traveling.

Teri had become comfortable in her own skin in the past decade, when she'd finally accepted that as long as she was fit and felt good, it wasn't necessary to be a stick. Oh, she wasn't fat. But like most women who'd had kids, her hips hadn't ever quite snapped back to where they were beforehand. And on the dark side of forty, she was starting to notice a certain propensity to softness, even with a religious workout schedule.

They finished setting things away in silence, then were left with nothing to keep them from awkwardly waiting for Emery to reappear. Trying not to stress about the coming talk with her son, Teri peeked at Aaron, after folding up her reusable bags to take home, and found him observing her intently.

"Sorry for the not-so-friendly greeting. You're not quite who I expected to find at the door," he finally volunteered.

Teri relaxed a bit as she smiled. "Now, you know I have to ask who you *did* expect."

Aaron grinned back, and something about him again struck her as familiar.

"Well, when Emery said his 'number one fan' was coming to spend the night, I thought he meant..." He trailed off, embarrassed, then gestured with a grimace. "You know, not a *mom*."

"Hmm. Guess I don't want to go there." She studied him, but his identity still didn't come to her. It was driving her crazy. "Aaron...Aaron..." she finally murmured aloud. "You look *really* familiar, but I just can't place you."

His smile dropped as if a curtain had fallen. He shrugged as a cloud passed over his eyes, negating the pleasant banter. It was such an abrupt change that Teri immediately regretted her nosy angling for information.

Without thought, she crossed to him and laid a hand on his arm. "I'm sorry. I didn't mean to pry."

Aaron took a deep breath and Teri felt his corded forearm flex under her touch. "No, *I'm* sorry. I overreacted. You're probably just thrown off by my name. They usually call me Hank." He met her eyes as they widened.

Teri straightened abruptly. *Of course!* Now everything snapped into place. 'Hank' Aaron Reynolds. Huge story after the live broadcast of his season — and possibly career — ending crash into the boards. Her eyes went straight to his right arm, knowing the reason he was on the Disabled List was the need for a long rehab of the shoulder of his throwing arm. The beautiful, ornate tattoo of a Celtic cross should have been a dead giveaway, except — her gaze shot in disbelief up to his spiky blond hair — he had cut his trademark shoulder-length hair. *No wonder I didn't know him.* It was — had been — his most recognizable feature.

And what was he even doing here? Teri battled to keep her pity and confusion from showing on her face. Playing in the *minors?* A member of last year's All-Star team?

Catching herself kneading his muscular forearm, she snatched her hand away and took several steps back — running into her son, who smelled of soap and shampoo, a vast improvement, and whom she hadn't even heard enter the room.

"You're Hank Reynolds?" Em had evidently drawn the same conclusions as she had about his new roommate. True to form, he then blurted out the biggest of the string of questions burning in her own mind, going on in a disbelieving tone, "Why're you going by Aaron? And what the fuck are you doing in the minors?"

Chapter Two

Aaron grimaced at the identical expressions of awe and shock from the matching amber eyes of mother and son.

You knew this was going to happen when you took this gig. It'll be a hundred times worse when the press finds out you're here.

He ran his hand over his hair in what was becoming a habitual manner, still unused to the short, close cut after over a decade of shoulder-length or longer. It had been an impulsive, symbolic gesture at the time of his surgery, to rid himself of the trademark hair while unable to play ball. But Aaron hadn't realized at the time just how anonymous it would make him. He'd gone from unable to leave his house without being recognized, to having fellow players and big fans have no idea who he was. While he didn't regret cutting it off exactly, he wondered if he'd ever regain his identity. And whether it even mattered to anyone besides himself.

Teri recovered first of the three of them. "Well, it's wonderful to meet you...Aaron." There was a very slight inflection trailing at the end, as if she was questioning the right name to use.

"Yeah. It's pretty much just the media and other ballplayers that call me Hank. And I'm not playing. I'm just here helping out Coach McCauley while I rehab." He shrugged, wincing as the automatic gesture pulled at his slow-healing surgical wound. "Better than just sitting around. And we're not sure how long this will take. It was a complicated injury."

That was an understatement. A chronic rotator cuff problem had plagued him since high school, when he'd been a pitcher, but he'd been able to put off surgery and nurse it along. Then a bad crash into the left field wall during the playoffs last fall had dislocated his shoulder and torn up some tendons to boot. All on his throwing side. And a left-fielder needed to be one-hundred percent with his gun.

The media hadn't yet got wind of the prevailing opinion among his rehab team that he might not get enough range of motion back to be able to play at his former level, if at all. So while he was officially still on his team's sixty-day-plus disabled list, he was fighting a losing battle coming into the start of the season, not yet ready to resume his position, but definitely not ready to give up on the only thing he'd ever wanted to do with his life—play ball.

Aaron clenched his jaw as he led the Sanduskys into the living room. He was only twenty-eight, damn it. He should've had another decade. And he *would*.

Mind firmly made up on that count, his eyes were drawn to Teri, curling up like a cat in the corner of the couch. When he'd opened the door, expecting to see some over-the-top baseball groupie, he'd been caught off guard by Teri's wholesome, unembellished beauty. A quick, hot flash of unexpected jealousy had spiked through him at the thought of her being here for Em and not him.

Aaron rolled his eyes. He should've known who she was right away by her coloring—a petite, feminine version of his new responsibility, with the same rich, dark hair and whiskey eyes. But no way did she look old enough to have a full-grown son. She was short—probably a foot shorter than his six-two—and fit, with a youthful, positive energy that radiated from her. With her hair pulled back into a long ponytail and no makeup to cover the smattering of freckles across her cheekbones and nose, she could walk around on a college campus without a second glance. He wouldn't be surprised if she still got carded for alcohol. Aaron frowned a bit as he wondered just how young she'd been when she'd had Emery.

Teri was currently directing a look at Emery that Aaron remembered being on the receiving end of a few times with his own parents, and he decided to make himself scarce for the coming clash.

"Sorry to bail, but I need to get my run in." Aaron turned to Teri and a conspiratorial shine in her eye told him she knew why he was heading out. Sharp lady. The more he saw of her, the more he liked.

He hurried to his bedroom and washed up, then laced his running shoes. He hadn't really planned on a run today, but he'd at least jog for a while and give the duo some privacy. Maybe he'd go down to the park and run by the river.

Aaron walked back out into the living room and Teri smiled at him when he appeared. There was just something about her…

He cleared his throat. "Make yourself at home. I'll be back in an hour or so."

"Thanks, Aaron. Have a good run." The sound of his real name on her lips continued to whisper in his head long after his departure.

As soon as the door closed behind Aaron, Teri turned to study Em. He stared back at her, his expression growing more defensive by the second.

Trying to keep things non-confrontational, she nonetheless opened with what was foremost in her mind. "You've only been here for one night—"

"Ma, I really don't need a lecture. So I went out with the guys. They were just welcoming me to the team."

"Until noon?" she asked wryly.

Emery had the grace to flush. He opened his mouth to speak, but she cut him off, *really* not wanting to hear anything about some groupie, or worse, a lie.

"Okay. Em, you're an adult. I don't have to agree with everything you do, any more than you have to answer to me for anything. Just…try to focus on what you came here for. All right? That's all I ask." She scooted closer to him on the couch and patted his jittering knee. "So, evidently you had no idea that Aaron was Hank Reynolds?"

As she'd intended, Emery relaxed and exclaimed, "I know! Oh my God. That's just crazy. I don't get it. And wow. I'm staying in Hank Reynolds' condo!" He dropped back against the cushion dramatically. "Though, I don't get why he has a condo here. But still." Emery sat back up with his typical energy and nearly bounced. "Hank Reynolds is my roommate. Whoa."

"Yeah. So you behave and be an extra-specially good roomie. Got it?" she ordered.

He nodded agreeably. "Got it. So how's Alex?"

She smiled at how eager Emery seemed to keep the subject off his behavior, and let it go for now. "He's good. Cross country just wrapped up with their last meet yesterday." Which was why she hadn't been able to come with Emery when he'd driven up with his belongings the day before, but Emery knew that. "He placed fifth, so a good showing. Busy with school and work, of course, with tax season." Alex had interned at a well-known accounting firm for the past year and now had a part-time, seasonal job as a tax preparer for them.

Emery rolled his eyes. "Boring. Dude needs to get a life."

That wasn't entirely inaccurate, but Teri would rather eat liver than admit it. Not for the first time, she wished she could give Em a bit of Alex's responsible nature, and Alex some of Emery's outgoing *joie de vivre*.

"He's happy. That's all I want for either of you."

Emery snorted. "He's not happy. He just has no social skills, so he hunkers down in his own little world."

"Em." Teri shook her head, refusing to get baited by her son's familiar taunting of his twin. "So what's the plan for today? We should probably get you unpacked." If he'd been out all night, she was sure he hadn't bothered to do any himself. She frowned. "The boxes aren't still out in the truck, are they?"

"Nah, we got them all inside."

"We? You didn't make Aaron help, did you? Not with a bad shoulder." She winced.

Emery had the grace to look guilty. "I had no idea about that at the time. And he offered," he defended.

"Okay, well, we'll need to be sure to do something nice for him. Maybe take him out to dinner tonight."

"Sure. That's a great idea, Ma. Some of the guys were saying that the burgers at this sports bar about ten minutes from here are really good."

Teri raised an eyebrow. "Burgers at a sports bar, huh? Is this meal for him or for you?"

"Hey, he's a guy. He has to like burgers, right?" Emery gave her a lopsided grin and she pursed her lips.

"Fine. Burgers it is, though from the looks of the fridge, he's a bit more serious about his nutrition than some people I know."

"Know and love," he teased.

"Yeah," she agreed and leaned forward to ruffle his damp hair. "This mop. I swear. I should cut your hair while I'm here."

"Ma! Come on…"

"Hard to field the ball when you have hair hanging in your face."

"That's what a hat's for."

Teri laughed. "Not exactly, but okay. Have it your way, Sasquatch." She rose from the couch and stretched her back, slightly stiff from the drive. "Let's take a look at your room and see what needs doing."

"Um…I have a better idea. Why don't I show you around? We'll go for a drive and I'll take you past the stadium, the grocery store, stuff like that."

Obviously, from his diversion tactic, his room was a mess, but she wasn't in the mood for a fight, and damned if she was going to do all the work while he bitched about unpacking on his last day off. "Okay, you win. But I *will* need a place to crash while I'm here, even if it's the couch, so we're going to have to tackle it sooner or later," she warned.

"Of course." His angelic smile at having got his way morphed into a more genuine one as he gave her an unexpected hug. "I'm glad to have you here, Ma."

Teri swallowed against the sudden lump in her throat. Emery wasn't nearly as demonstrative as Alex, and was far more independent lately. It was beyond nice to actually hear that from her distractible son.

Rather than answer, she hugged him back. Maybe this would be a positive experience and place for him after all.

Chapter Three

"Hey, Brighton!" Emery yelled over the din of the pub, gesturing to a trio of players Aaron recognized from the team.

Aaron, Teri and Emery had lingered for hours over dinner at the sports bar Emery had chosen for their meal out, and while Emery had only had one beer in front of his mom during dinner, Aaron knew that the group approaching were among the wilder guys on the team, which most likely spelled the end of Em's restraint. He shook his head. Had he ever been that young and stupid?

Easy answer—no way. He had been too grateful to get the shot at professional ball to screw it up.

Emery slung an arm around Teri in an easy, familiar manner as the guys boisterously greeted them, pulling up chairs around their table. Aaron envied their close relationship, so different from his upbringing.

"This is Teri," Emery introduced her to the guys joining them.

"Very nice, Dusky. But she looks too classy for the likes of you." Chet Brighton leaned across the table, reaching for Teri's hand. "How about you forget about Emery here, and let me buy you a drink?"

The sight of the player's hand about to touch Teri's set off a clamor of anger in Aaron, but before he could react, Teri withdrew her hand to a safe distance as Emery spoke up.

"What the hell, Chet? She's my freaking mom. Get your paws off her."

The other two guys were laughing hysterically as Chet backed off, scowling at Emery for a moment before turning the charm back on. "Fine by me. I like older women, and I'll even forgive you for having this joker for a son. I'm sure you did all you could in raising him." He sent a practiced, smoldering look her way that had Aaron rolling his eyes.

Teri gave a sweet smile. "Nice to meet you, Chet. If I see any desperate older women, I'll definitely send them your way." She turned to Aaron and Emery. "Are you guys ready to head home?"

Amused by her deft manner at putting the kid in his place, Aaron glanced from Teri to Emery.

Mitch Williams protested, "Hey, it's early. You guys aren't calling it a night already? We're on our way to The Billboard—they have a live DJ tonight."

"C'mon, Ma," Emery encouraged. "You know you want to go dancing." He nudged her playfully.

Aaron and Teri locked gazes, and he shrugged, wanting to leave the decision up to her since he was their ride home. He really wasn't up for a night of babysitting this motley crew, but had to admit the idea of seeing Teri moving on the dance floor held undeniable appeal. Her sparkling eyes searched his for a long moment before she turned to her son.

"Okay, but remember I turn into a pumpkin at midnight."

* * * *

The Billboard was warm and packed. Aaron wedged his way up to the bar while the other players disappeared into the crowd and Teri and Emery headed straight onto the dance floor. He ordered a bottle of water then took it to a vacant spot along the railing surrounding the dance area. With the height of the players, he was able to immediately spot Emery and, less visibly, Teri among the gyrating forms. He slid along the rail, trying for a better view.

There.

Teri was lost in the rhythm, swiveling and swaying with the music. Aaron's mouth went dry as he ran his gaze down her slender back to those curvaceous, circling hips, effortlessly keeping the beat as she danced in front of Emery. They moved around, and now Aaron had a look at her joyous face, laughing up at her son.

Suddenly, her eyes lowered from Emery's face and locked on Aaron's gaze from across the room. If anything, her smile got wider and his pulse leaped as she crooked her finger to beckon him. He was sure the gesture was meant to be convivial rather than sexual, but his increasingly interested body made its own interpretation. Without conscious thought, he set down his water and threaded his way through the crowd, receiving a few blatant touches and even more looks. Aaron disregarded them all, completely focused on Teri, and he began to dance as he reached the pair.

Aaron loved to dance and it was easy to give himself over to the pounding music. If anything, Teri looked even smaller in the midst of the chaos on the dance floor, and Aaron glided closer, until there was barely air between them. Emery had turned away and had his arms wrapped around a tall blonde from behind, grinding into her. Aaron was left to partner with Teri, and they moved together well into the next song before he finally gave in to his rising need to touch her.

The first contact was three fingers lightly resting on the waistband of her jeans, just above her hip. As she raised her arms above her head, her shirt lifted just enough so the tip of Aaron's finger found bare, warm flesh. Awareness sizzled through him, and he could feel his body react, his cock thickening slowly, inexorably.

Teri's face was upturned to his, her lips parted, and he knew she was sharing his arousal as they moved together in public foreplay. She placed her hand on his forearm and he recalled how her touch in the kitchen earlier had taken him right out of his funk and ignited the first spark of attraction for her. Not as the mom of his roommate, or ally in his fight to keep Emery on the straight and narrow, but as a vital, desirable woman.

Aaron imagined covering her small body with his and rocking into her heat, and he groaned. It had been a long time since he'd had such an immediate attraction to anyone. He moved even closer, setting subtlety aside and firmly grasping her hips. His knees were bent slightly, framing hers as they danced. Her pelvis just barely rode his thigh, and he made little thrusts in time to the music, mimicking the very act he was now envisioning.

Teri's hand curled around the back of his neck, sliding into the short, freshly cut hair there, and it felt so good, Aaron closed his eyes to savor the contact. For the first time, he was glad to have his new, short haircut. Her exploration was at once thrilling and soothing. They continued to move together as if they'd been partnering together for years, and Aaron forgot about the crowd, forgot about Emery—forgot everything except the beat and the feel of the woman molded against him. He pressed as close to Teri as he could and still maintain the outward appearance of dancing and rejoiced at the answering, accepting brush of her jaw against his chest.

The dance mix went on and on, melding from one song into the next, fast and slow, and Aaron and Teri continued to move together as if one. Eventually the DJ took a break, and Aaron was brought abruptly to the surface from his absorption in Teri and looked around at the clearing dance floor. He was irritated, but not surprised, to find that Emery had disappeared from view.

Teri looked up at him wryly. "Back to reality?" she teased.

"And looks like we lost our third," he observed, a bit chagrined at how completely he had lost himself.

He placed a hand on her warm lower back as they walked toward the edge of the dance floor. Teri had her phone out and was texting rapidly. Aaron barely heard the answering chime.

Rather than tell him the response, Teri held the screen up to show Aaron.

Last minute thing. Don't wait up.

"Well, I guess he must have a ride." Aaron suddenly felt awkward as he looked down at the woman to whom he'd been intimately glued for the past hour, the woman he would be taking home tonight…

Without the bass-heavy beat pushing them together, he was starting to second-guess the wisdom of giving in to his attraction for her. Between his obligation to the team, the impermanence of his time here and having to live with Emery, he saw nothing but complications ahead if he were to get involved with Teri.

Despite the best efforts of his brain to reign in his wayward body, he ran his eyes over her compact form.

Teri met his regard and gave him a knowing look in return. Casually taking his hand in hers, she tugged and invited, "Let's go home."

Chapter Four

What are you doing, girl?

Without Emery's chattering presence, the ride back to Aaron's condo was quiet and gave Teri plenty of time to re-examine every nuance of the evening. She refused to answer her own scolding thoughts, while trying her best to tamp down her libido. Their dance, aka public sex, had roused her well past fever pitch, and she was relieved — and a bit surprised — she hadn't come right out on the dance floor.

Seriously, he's almost young enough to be your son!

Well, not quite. She'd done a quick, furtive Google search under the table at dinner and had confirmed that Aaron was a respectable twenty-eight. Almost twenty-nine, even. Only a bit over ten years difference, if rounded down. And why not? Fourteen was closer to ten than twenty.

He was in grade school when the boys were born!

Point?

No point, really, except it had been a while since Teri had connected with anyone. For some reason, she'd always been drawn to young, confident guys in their twenties. Now that there was a 'four' in front of her age, she was beginning to wonder how appropriate that preference was. But she knew besides the obvious plus of having sexy guys in their physical prime, the younger set were a better fit with her lifestyle.

Guys her age invariably had baggage, serious expectations or didn't share her interests. She had enough of her own baggage to haul around, thank you very much, without the addition of someone else's failed marriage or kids. And she wasn't looking for a serious relationship, something older men looking for wife number two — or three — didn't understand. Teri had worked hard to raise her kids alone, earn her degree and put in her time in the coal mines until she could support herself with freelance work. Now she could travel to Emery's games, take jobs when it suited her and have the freedom she'd never got to experience back as a young adult. She wasn't about to give her hard-earned lifestyle up for anyone.

Teri enjoyed the sight of Aaron's well-built frame preceding her up the stairs to his condo. She ran her gaze down his v-shaped back, his shirt — still damp from the dancing — clinging to it, revealing every mouth-watering detail. And speaking of mouth-watering... Her gaze drifted down to his taut, muscled ass and thighs, temptingly displayed in his tight, worn jeans.

She ran a hand along her pelvis as she climbed the stairs and cupped herself hard, trying to alleviate the tingling in her pussy. The memory of riding that hard thigh at the dance club, feeling the pressure in just the right spot, had her wanting to climb back on and finish the job. *And why not?* Aaron was, as far as she knew, free to indulge. She snatched her hand away and tried to look innocent as he turned from unlocking the door.

"So, Aaron, how do you like living here? Met anyone?" Inwardly, she winced. That was a little obvious. But then again, she didn't have much time to waste on subtlety. She needed to get back home in a couple of days.

The question seemed to catch Aaron off-guard. He paused on the way to the kitchen, then continued on his way, calling back, "I'm actually really familiar with it, since I lived here when I was in the minors. That's when I bought this condo." He came back in with two chilled water bottles. "Water?"

She accepted it, grateful for his consideration, and they moved to the couch. She kicked off her shoes and curled up almost in the middle and, after a moment, Aaron joined her, just a short reach away.

"So you just kept it then?" she asked, interested in why he would still own this simple apartment when he lived in a different city.

Aaron shrugged. "I just never took for granted that I'd be up in the majors for the long haul. Even after I bought my condo there, I decided to keep this one and let Coach rent it out cheap to guys on the team here." He took a few long swallows of water, his throat working, and her eyes were drawn helplessly to the motion.

"How about you? It's the work week, but you're able to get away...?" he prompted.

Teri shrugged. "I do a hodgepodge of consulting, quality control and auditing for medical practices. So I can pretty much schedule myself however I like. Believe me, it took a long time to get that kind of flexibility, but now that I have it, I love it." She relaxed against the cushion, and Aaron mirrored her, leaning back as well, their shoulders nearly touching. "It lets me keep up with Emery's schedule and get to all his away games. And, of course, the CWS in June. I go every year." She animatedly gestured as she referred to the College World Series. "And then pro games when I get a chance all summer and fall." She paused to take a deep breath.

"You really like baseball, don't you?" Aaron grinned.

She couldn't help but respond to his gorgeous smile and close proximity, and did what she'd been dying to do since he'd opened the door in his workout clothes. She kissed him, just a brush at first, and his surprised exhalation fanned her cheeks as she deepened the kiss and swung her leg over his lap to straddle him.

His hands came up to bracket her hips as she ran hers into his trimmed hair, so silky to the touch, even short as it was. It must've been heavenly when it was long, and the thought had her clenching her fingers in what remained, dragging a groan from him as he engaged in the kiss.

One arm snaked around the back of her waist, trapping her in an iron grip. Meanwhile Aaron's other hand skimmed the back of her scalp, snapping the barrette open then working into her hair, spreading it out along her back and over her shoulder.

All the while he was kissing her breathless, his mouth slanting in demand over hers, taking all control away from her, control she was happy to cede as long as it kept him pressing against her, soothing the ache that had been building all day. Her tongue met his and they slid together, learning each other's true taste, sharing breath.

Aaron pulled back a little and she made a needy, pleading noise under her breath. But he only separated enough to watch his hand as it trailed down her hair, stopping just above the peak of her breast.

"Beautiful," he murmured as he gave short, teasing strokes over her loosened hair, the heat and touch penetrating to stop just short of her begging nipple each pass. She arched into the touch, trying to force contact, and at last he complied, cupping her fullness and running his thumb over the hardening peak.

She huffed out a breath of relief and pressed fully against his hard chest, trapping his hand just where she wanted it while she coasted her open lips along his jawline, the rough growth against her mouth sending shivers through her. His taste was salty and warm on her tongue as she darted it out to sample the skin of his neck. A sensuous smile rose to her lips as he tilted his head to give her better access. She took full advantage, nibbling and sucking lightly down to that sexy spot where neck and shoulder met. There she concentrated her efforts, drinking in his scent, careful not to make a mark, but teasing with her teeth and tongue as she felt his cock filling against her groin.

She rotated her hips against him and he reacted with breathtaking speed, standing up with her still twined around him. Teri gasped and clutched at him as he rose, then had the air whoosh out of her lungs as he turned and dropped her on her back onto the couch, landing atop her, snug in the cradle of her thighs.

His beautiful light green eyes were just inches away, gazing warmly into hers.

"Hi," he whispered. "Comfy?"

"Oh, yeah." Teri squirmed a tad to get the fit against him just right. "Very comfy. You?"

"Perfect."

His answer lingered in the silence as the implication in the tone of his voice made clear he was speaking of much more than his position. She watched as his eyes traced every nuance of her face from up close, and felt a brief dart of self-consciousness, knowing that her freckles and laugh lines were probably all too evident at this range.

"Perfect," he repeated, a bit more forceful, apparently noticing her moment of doubt. A sudden burst of affection for Aaron had her giving him a tight hug, genuine and nonsexual despite their intimate position. Teri had really enjoyed his company all day. He was a likeable guy once she'd managed to get past his reserve. She figured his cool front had probably come from dealing with his media fame.

She studied his familiar face. To Teri, as with everyone who followed baseball, he had been very recognizable—a larger than life, but two-dimensional figure—before today. Someone seen in highlight clips, official photos and sports magazine spreads. Now, out of uniform and with his hair cut short, he seemed so much more human, real and touchable. She wondered how many people saw this side of him.

She was observing him closely, so she noticed the very slight wince as he shifted above her.

"Are you okay?"

He looked surprised then regretful. "It's my shoulder, I have to—" He began to lever himself up with his good arm.

"Oh! Of course." She helped push him up with her hands on his chest, instantly missing the feel of his weight pressing her down into the cushions. She scooted up and backwards into a sitting position as he settled next to her, lifting his good arm and looking at her in invitation.

"How's that?" she asked, fitting herself against his side, snuggling in.

"*Almost* perfect?" He quirked his lips as he waited for her reaction then yelped as Teri elbowed him. "Ouch! You have sharp elbows."

Teri snickered as she soothed his abused side with a gentle stroke of her hand, completely at ease. She continued to pet him as she rested her head against his chest. How was it that she was so comfortable with Aaron so soon?

It had been a long time since she'd had someone to cuddle with, that's for sure. And Aaron was very affectionate. She recalled the gentle pressure to her back as he'd guided her, the way he had gravitated toward her on the couch. Very touchy-feely, obviously comfortable with it, and she was the same way. It was nice—more than nice—to be with someone who enjoyed contact as much as she did. Teri was soaking it up, and it looked as though it was feeding a need for Aaron as well.

And speaking of feeding a need…

Teri reached over to grasp Aaron's forearm, giving a hard squeeze, which startled a huff of laughter out of Aaron.

"What are you doing?" His eyes twinkled down at her and she grinned back.

"I've been dying to do that all day." She continued to learn the feel of that corded, muscled arm, her touch trailing over the crisp, light hair. God, he was incredible. She'd always had a thing for powerful arms, and after playing ball for as long as he had, he had them in spades. "Damn, feel those pipes."

Unbelievably, Aaron went beet red. Okay, that was just too cute.

"Am I embarrassing you?" Teri teased, leaning forward for a better look at his flushed face, hand still caressing his arm.

"Yes" — he laughed — "and my first instinct is to throw you back down on the couch, but you know how well that worked out last time."

It had certainly worked for her anyway. She thought for a moment. "We don't want you to get hurt again, so let's do this instead." Teri stood, reluctantly letting go of her prize, and began to encourage Aaron to lie down on his good side. As he realized what she was up to, his eyes lit up and he arranged himself to accommodate her. Teri wasted no time in spooning with him, and the feel of his long, warm body wrapped around her lulled her into utter contentment.

Well, most of her.

She wriggled and he groaned in her ear. "Will you settle down?"

"Sorry," she responded, unrepentant. "All that dancing wound me up."

"If you still feel like dancing..." Aaron slowly slid his hand across her abdomen and slid it down to cup her sex, just like she had earlier on the stairs, but oh, stars. His touch was much different, larger, warmer, urging her back against his growing erection. She reached behind her with her hand, finding his scalp as she tilted her head to expose her neck to his kiss.

Aaron stroked his long fingers over her core, and she was instantly frustrated by the layers of clothing between his touch and her flesh. Zeroing in on her clit, he tapped and pressed, the sensation muted by her jeans, and now it was her turn to groan as she shamelessly threw her leg over the top of his thigh, opening to his exploration.

His hand left her for a moment and she canted her head back in disbelief. Then those nimble fingers were at the top button of her jeans, working it open then easing the zipper down.

Teri held her breath and pulled in her stomach, pussy clenching in anticipation, expecting a zig as he again zagged and abandoned her lower body. Disappointed, she made a frustrated noise in her throat, prompting a low chuckle from behind her.

"I gotcha," he promised, and found his way under her shirt. She gave a smile as he paused and sucked in a breath as he discovered her braless state. Every touch and slide of his hand against her bare skin was heavenly and her nipples were like cut diamonds, almost painful as they begged for soothing.

Humming with pleasure, she undulated against him as he plucked and teased her breasts, alternating between cupping then running his palm over their curves. Surging against her ass, he met her rhythm and she finally needed to take more. She flipped halfway over, onto her back, leaving her body open to his whims while allowing her access to his zipper.

She glanced up, arrested by the heated look on his handsome face as they worked together to open his jeans. Unimpeded by underwear—*oh, gads, he goes commando?*—his cock sprang out into her palm as if dying for her touch, silky warmth over steel. She closed her fingers around him as he delved into her jeans and found her slick center.

"Ahh," she gasped as he used her own juices to make his pass over her clit almost unbearably perfect. She licked her palm with as much spit as she could manage then returned her hand to his hot erection as he took her mouth in a torrid kiss.

Both of them were on edge from the dancing and the foreplay, and Teri knew it wouldn't take long for him to bring her over the top, not with his knowing, demanding caress. It was just what she needed. She strove for the pinnacle, working her hand over his cock as she arched into his touch. Milking pre-cum from the head, using it to help her gliding grip, she writhed helplessly and panted into his mouth.

The continuous groan emanating from his throat suddenly cut off then intensified as the length in her hand grew even harder. Then warmth spilled over her hand. She tensed and was there with him, tossing her head back as she crested and peaked. Aaron's mouth stilled on hers but he didn't move away as they shared the moment of bliss along with their very breath as they floated in descent.

Teri opened her eyes — when had she closed them? — and Aaron was watching her with a pleased and sated expression, his handsome face almost slack with repletion, other than the slight smile quirking one corner of his luscious lips. As she held his gaze, she raised her hand and ran her tongue along the side of her finger, gathering his cum for a taste.

His eyebrows shot up, but he recovered quickly as he gave her tender clit one last, unbearable stroke before bringing his own finger up to suck off her essence.

Then they were both laughing and kissing. Teri burrowed into his chest, not able to get close enough. She heaved a contented sigh.

"Wow." Aaron's chest rumbled under her with his voice. "Haven't made out on the couch like that in years. That was fun. Like being a teenager again."

"That wasn't *that* long ago for you. Wait'll you get to my age," she scolded, feeling a bit put out at the reference to age right that minute.

Aaron gave her a hard hug. "Hey. Don't start getting hung up on age. I can't help when I was born."

"True," she conceded, deciding to let it go for now. A yawn snuck up on her. "We'd better get off the couch before we fall asleep here."

"A few more minutes?" Aaron tempted as he gently stroked her arm.

Yes, she was tempted all right. But the last thing she wanted was for Emery to come in and find her all tangled up with a man — especially his roommate.

"Nope, up and at 'em." She did a controlled roll off the couch then stood and fastened her jeans, easily evading Aaron's half-hearted attempt to grab her ass. She paused for a second as a thought occurred to her. "Unless this is my bed for tonight. Either way, you need to get up."

Aaron stood and tucked himself back into his jeans, making a show of being disgruntled. "I put clean sheets on his bed this afternoon for you to use, so actually this is Emery's bed tonight. Oops." He checked the cushions. "Looks like we were careful."

Teri snorted. "Oh shit, well, that's good. And thanks for making the bed. I was going to get to it..." A bit shy now that the tension between them had finally been banked, she fell back on her humor, giving him a teasing look over her shoulder as she preceded him down the hall. "At least we should both sleep well tonight now."

Aaron stopped and pulled her back into his arms. "Sleep with me tonight."

And oh, wasn't that a decadent thought? How long had it been since she'd slept with strong arms wrapped around her? Conflicted, the war inside her was won by her customary self-denial. "Better not. Not that I don't want to," she hastily assured him as his face dropped a bit. "But let's just call it a night. Okay?"

Aaron was nodding before she finished speaking. "Okay. But if you change your mind…" He trailed off, indicating his bedroom door.

"You'll be the first to know," she finished lightly. "I had fun tonight," she added, dawdling. Now that the time had come, she hated to part from him. Teri forced herself to open the door to Emery's room and step inside. "Night, Aaron."

"Night, Teri. Glad to have you."

She closed the door and leaned back against it, feeling her heart pound as the innuendo in his goodnight added an almost physical touch to his words. "I'll be glad to have you, too," she whispered with a smile, looking forward to sweet dreams.

Chapter Five

Teri stretched herself awake, feeling sated and happy. Oh, yes, pleasant dreams indeed. Wow, Aaron was something else. She squirmed as she remembered how expertly and unselfishly he'd brought her to pleasure last night. She opened her eyes, looking around in vain for a clock, and felt her good mood take a slight dip as she noticed the state of Emery's room. *Back to reality, Mom.* Boxes were stacked haphazardly, piles of clothes everywhere. Guess she would be doing some unpacking today or it would likely never get done.

She peeked out into the hall, then padded to the bathroom to get herself ready for the day. It was very quiet so either everyone was still sleeping or they'd already gone to practice.

Teri was just finished getting dressed as she heard the landline ring. Walking out into the living room, she listened to it ring a few times before it went to the machine. Nobody home then. She headed to the kitchen to see whether Aaron was a coffee drinker or if she needed to make a trip out.

As the message began, she heard Aaron's voice coming from the machine. "Teri? If you're there, please pick up."

She quickly crossed to the phone and lifted the receiver. "Hey, Aaron. Good morning," she added huskily, eyes finally landing on the stovetop clock. Ten oh nine. Jeez, she'd slept in. No wonder she felt so good.

"Is Emery there?"

Teri frowned and walked out into the living room. It looked just the same as when they'd gone to bed the night before. No shoes by the door or keys on the entry table. "No, it doesn't look like it. Are you at practice?"

"Yes, just started at ten, but Emery's not here yet." He blew out a breath. "McCauley is pretty strict about the guys being punctual, so I wanted to try to get him here before they notice he's missing. Damn it!" Aaron's frustration was evident in his voice, and it reflected her own rising ire.

"I'll try his phone. Maybe if he hears my ringtone, he'll get a frickin' clue," she snapped then softened. "Thanks, Aaron, Em's lucky to have you watching his back. Maybe he'll start actually appreciating it himself one of these days."

The edge vanished from his tone. "Sorry for the abrupt awakening. Hey, I've got to get going. I'm going to track down Mitch and Chet to see if they know where he went." Aaron sighed. "Call me if you get hold of him." As he rattled off his cell number, she grabbed a pen and wrote it on her hand.

"Got it." Teri hung up and found her phone. No messages. She hit Em's speed dial and waited, tapping her foot.

Just before it went to voicemail, she heard his voice, still groggy from sleep. "Ma?"

"Emery Paul! Where are you? Never mind. You need to get to practice, right now. It's after ten."

"Shit!" There was a loud clunk as Em apparently dropped the phone, and Teri heard some rustling and the murmur of a feminine voice.

Oh, great.

"Emery. Em!" she called, and he came back on the line.

"What, Ma? I've gotta get dressed." His voice was muffled as if he were holding it to his ear with his shoulder.

"Do you have a ride and everything you need?"

"Yeah, I have a ride. Oh, fuck, my bag—equipment. It's still in my truck. I think I have some workout clothes in there…"

Teri was already grabbing her purse and keys. "I'll meet you there." She shook her head, sliding into her sport sandals. *Whatever.* "We have a lot to discuss, kiddo, so don't even *think* about making any plans for tonight. *Capiche?*" With that, she hung up.

She hustled out of the apartment, locked up behind her then went down the stairs, wondering where the hell Emery had parked so she could grab his gear.

Finally locating Emery's pickup, she decided to just go ahead and take it instead of moving his stuff to her own car.

She hopped in and checked that, yes, his bags were behind the seat. She leaned over, unzipped the duffle bag and was relieved to spy some clothes and cleats. They might not be clean but whatever. Irritated by the abrupt and frustrating turn to what had started out as a nice day, she bounced into the seat and adjusted it forward until she could reach the pedals. She started the engine, and rolled her eyes. Not only was the oil light on, the fuel gauge rested just above empty. Typical.

Great. Hopefully I won't run out of gas.

Before she pulled out, she dialed Aaron.

"Hello?"

"Hey, it's me. He's on his way, and so am I since his stuff is all in his truck."

Aaron blew out a breath. "Thanks, Teri." Aaron sounded relieved but had a hint of disgust in his voice. "Good thing our group started with conditioning instead of field time today. He might actually get away with it, but this has got to stop."

"I agree. Believe me, we'll be having a 'come to Jesus' tonight."

Aaron snorted dismissively. "Well, you already had one yesterday, which didn't exactly do the trick. Not sure how effective more talking's going to be."

Teri prickled as the not-so-subtle dig at her parenting hit home. "Wow, thanks for throwing that back in my face. I'll see you later. I have to drive now."

"Teri—"

His voice was cut off satisfyingly as she hung up on him.

* * * *

She was still steaming when she pulled up to the stadium just in time to see Emery unfolding himself from the passenger's seat of a red Miata. Teri pulled in right behind him and was somewhat mollified to see a relieved and grateful expression on his face as he spotted her. She threw the truck into park, left it running and hopped out.

Emery hurriedly said goodbye to whoever was in the car and hustled over. He reached past her through the driver's door grab his equipment bag and his duffle out of backseat area of the cab. "Thanks, Ma. I'm so sorry—"

"Don't thank me—thank Aaron. He's the one who got the search party going. Now get in there before you're missed." She swatted his butt, hard. He jumped but wisely didn't say anything. "Go!" she prodded.

He headed for the stadium at a run, and she watched him until he'd disappeared from view, then got back into the truck. She sat for a few minutes, letting the adrenaline drain from her, leaving her feeling tired and every year of her age. Her gaze landed on the fuel light. Fuck. She'd better gas up before her day got even worse.

She went toward a gas station she'd spotted on the way there, and while she was waiting to turn left, her phone chimed with a text. By the time she'd pulled up to the pumps, another one hit.

Figuring it was either Em or maybe Aaron, she ignored them, and got out to fill the tank. That was the limit of her restraint, though, and her curiosity got the better of her by the time she'd grabbed the receipt and got back in.

She glanced at her phone, and one was from Aaron.

Thanks for getting him here. Coach noticed. Not happy. Might be late getting home.

Wonderful. She sighed and since she couldn't think of a polite reply, and didn't really want to talk to him anyway after the criticism earlier, she moved on to the next text, this one from Alex.

Were you at the party with Em last night or did he sneak out? LOL. Check FB.

She had no desire to see whatever was on Facebook, but she did answer this one.

He escaped when we went dancing. I look away for one second... Sigh.

Well, it had been more than a second that she'd been distracted. She shifted on the seat as the memory of last night brought back a pleasant residual ache. Her phone rang with Alex's ringtone.

"Hi, honey."

"Hey, Ma. What's wrong? Em giving you a hard time?"

Alex had always been so in tune with her moods. Even as a young boy, he'd seemed to know exactly what she was thinking.

"Yeah, sort of. I really don't want to talk about your brother right now, though."

"Okay, but you know I'm here if you need me."

"Thanks, Alex." Older than his years. She thought about his schedule. "Don't you have class right now?"

"It was canceled because the prof is sick, but I didn't get the message, I guess. I'm walking back to the apartment now, so I thought I'd check in and see how it was going with you, especially after the pics I saw..." He paused. "Sorry, I know you don't want to talk about Em. Anyway, I might go in and see if I can help out at the office—"

"You should take the extra time and chill out, doing something relaxing or fun."

"I already went for a run this morning."

"I meant besides running. Maybe go to a movie? Go shopping? Have lunch?"

"Seriously, Ma. By myself, at ten-thirty in the morning?"

"Oh." That was true. "I was just thinking you spend enough time working, studying and working out. I worry that you're not enjoying the rest of what college is about."

"I'm fine, you don't need to worry. It's not like I'm a hermit or anything. I go out."

"Hmm."

"I do! Hey, save your mental energy for the other one. My life is under control. Okay?" Alex reassured her.

Under a bit too much control, actually. She sighed, not really sure she should be complaining about that. "Okay, hon." She glanced up as someone pulled in behind her at the pump. "I'd better move—just gassed up Em's truck and I'm blocking the pumps."

"Typical," he echoed her thought from earlier and she laughed. He joined in, and her tension eased. She couldn't be *that* bad of a mom if Alex had turned out so well. Em was a good kid, too, just...well...a bit too much of a kid for his age and this opportunity.

"Talk soon," she promised.

"Love you. Say hey to the brat for me."

"Will do. Bye."

"Bye."

Despite the pleasant conversation with Alex, Teri's frustration returned when she got back to the apartment and took another look at the boxes and garbage sacks of clothes in his room. *What am I going to do with Em?* He had an opportunity here that thousands of guys would kill for and he was happy to just fuck around. She went over scenario after scenario in her head as she put herself into work mode, trying to come up with something to motivate him.

Chapter Six

By the time late afternoon rolled around, she had settled dozens of recriminations on herself for failing as his mom. In the meantime, she had, ironically enough, been a mom in overdrive. She'd done a quick inventory then had gone back out to get a few more things at the store, and while she was out she'd gotten an oil change and washed his truck. She'd unpacked all of his clothes and most of the boxes and arranged his room, then fixed his favorite pea and cheese salad to go with the steaks she had marinating.

Pissed off or not, she didn't want to be spiteful about it, and she always felt better when she was getting things done. Standing with her hands on her hips, she took a last look around Emery's room. Part of her was cynically wondering whether she'd just be packing it all back up again soon, but maybe having a more settled space would somehow make him work to stay.

Teri had racked her brain trying to come up with the perfect combination of words to convince Emery to take this once-in-a-lifetime shot seriously. She was at a loss, though, so she'd soon given up and tried to clear her mind. It kept drifting back to the unexpected, sexy evening she'd spent with Aaron the night before.

It would bubble up in her brain now and then who he really was, and it was odd trying to reconcile the famous ballplayer with the man whose touch had brought out a side of her she'd never really known before. As much as she loved ball, she'd never been a groupie—and really, she hadn't exactly had a chance to be young and focused on anything so carefree as hooking up, at least not after that first time. So to her, he was just Aaron. And last night had been beyond hot, though his crack about her ineffective lecture this morning had stung.

Maybe she should cut him some slack. He'd never been a parent, so he probably had no idea how personal it felt when someone criticized how she treated her kids. If the topic even came up, perhaps she'd liken it to someone hacking on his ball playing or training regime.

Actually, she should just let it drop. A few days from now, she'd be back home. And while she'd continue to make the trips up to see Emery play, they'd be sporadic and short. The team would be on the road, she'd have work and eventually Aaron would be rejoining his own team…if Emery didn't get cut before then.

She heaved a sigh and sat down on the bed. Basically she just had to get along with him on the surface of things until their ways parted for good. No one was forcing them to spend time with one another, and two people certainly didn't have to have every little thing in agreement in order to have sex. Good sex. Really amazing…

Stop it.

Teri's gaze landed on the boxes, and she jumped up, glad to have one more task to distract her from her mental spiral. She could finish that then clean herself up and maybe check email or something until the guys got back.

She was just hauling a stack of broken down and folded up boxes out to her car, thinking longingly of a nice, hot shower, when Aaron and Emery pulled up into Aaron's parking space.

Crap. And here she looked like shit, and frankly didn't feel like talking to either one of them.

Briefly considering ignoring them both, she nodded toward them as they got out and approached, and continued without pausing toward her car.

"There's a recycling bin over there." There was a subdued note to Aaron's voice as he gestured to the enclosed dumpster area.

"I'll just take them home for now. You never know when you might suddenly need moving boxes." She stared pointedly at Emery. He apparently got the reference since he swallowed hard, but he held his tongue and simply took the boxes from her. He walked silently next to her, placed them in the trunk of her car then headed upstairs without a word, leaving Teri and Aaron alone.

Teri chanced a look at Aaron. The chastened look on his face hit home. Whether it was the sudden exhaustion from working all day, or her mental struggle over what to do with her son, she stupidly needed reassurance. She took a slow step toward him, then another. Suddenly they were moving into each other's arms.

"I'm sorry, babe." Aaron held her tight. He ran his hand over her hair then toyed with her ponytail. "That was a really shitty thing to say, especially right then.

Not exactly supportive. I shouldn't have taken my frustration with Emery out on you. I felt horrible all day."

"No, you were actually right. Talking doesn't seem to work with him," Teri conceded. She sighed into his chest, enjoying the feeling of giving up her cares for the moment. "I just don't know what to do."

"Well, Coach McCauley and Ron, one of the assistant coaches, had Emery in their office for a long time after practice today, that's why we're back so late."

She pulled back, though his arms remained lightly around her waist. "Oh no! What did they say?"

Aaron grimaced and moved so they were strolling slowly toward the stairs, his hand riding lightly on her lower back. "He wouldn't tell me, but Ron said Coach ripped him a new one. Said talent only goes so far and they didn't have time to waste on prima donnas who disrespect their coaches and teammates like he has been."

Teri winced. "Ouch. No wonder he was so quiet." Her heart ached for her baby boy. A dressing down like that from a respected authority figure, well-earned or not, had to have hurt.

"I caught hell too, for not rounding him up earlier."

What? Teri stopped moving and stared at him. "That's not fair. He's an adult, he's responsible for himself." She thought about what she'd just said, gave a wry laugh and qualified, "Well, technically." And she would do well to remember that he was a grown up. She wouldn't do either one of them any favors by bailing him out of situations. He had to stand on his own two feet, even if that meant she sometimes had to watch him fall.

It was still hard, though. Occasionally she thought that the hardest part of parenting was knowing when to stop.

She was relieved when Aaron winked. "Don't worry about it. Both my job here and my babysitting gig are voluntary on my part." He turned them back toward the stairs, throwing an arm around her shoulders.

"Ick, I'm all sweaty," she protested, trying to pull away. The feel of his arm across her damp T-shirt forcibly brought back to her how disgusting she was. He refused to let go, and she acquiesced without a struggle, remembering his shoulder.

"So am I," he reminded her. "I showered up after my rehab session and weights, but didn't take a second one after helping run outfield practice. I'd just as soon clean up at home." He let her go as they entered the apartment door Emery had left ajar. The sounds of a shower running came down the hall.

"Sounds like Emery beat you to it."

A warm shaft of desire shot through her as he suddenly cupped her ass in both hands and pulled her flush against him.

"Wanna shower with me?"

Teri's eyes widened as the wet and wonderful possibilities flashed like an X-rated movie trailer in her head. She nibbled her lower lip as she found herself hard-pressed to say no.

Looking like he'd just won the lottery, Aaron grinned wide. "Seriously? You're considering it?" He abruptly let go of her ass then encircled one wrist as he turned away. She stumbled to keep up as he pulled her down the hall to his room, leading her inside and closing the door before she could protest.

He yanked his damp shirt over his head, then tossed it toward a hamper by a door she assumed led to the en suite bathroom. When he hooked his thumbs in the waistband of his now-tented pants, she held up a hand.

"Whoa. We can't do this," Teri whispered urgently, dying to see more of him in the light of day, but very conscious of her son just down the hall.

Sure we can... Her body was all in favor of the idea.

"Sure we can, if you hurry up," he persuaded. "You should know better than anyone he takes forever in the shower. C'mon." He beckoned, backing toward the bathroom. "C'mon, Teri," he repeated in a low, sexy rumble. His gaze was locked on hers and she had to fight to keep from taking a step toward him.

It wasn't as though Em was going to search her out anytime soon. In fact, she'd be lucky if she got him out of his room to eat dinner. So really, there was nothing keeping her from indulging. Just two consenting adults...

"Just...wait." She held up her hand and watched him make an effort try to smooth his features as he battled his disappointment. That show of maturity and restraint more than anything made up her mind for her.

She whipped her own shirt over her head and watched his jaw drop.

"Okay, *now* you can take off your pants."

Chapter Seven

Aaron's erection came roaring back to life at the unexpected vision of Teri's small but perfect, pink-tipped breasts as she stood topless, hands on hips, waiting impatiently for him to strip. He tried to catch up mentally. He'd just been joking when he'd first suggested a shower together, but then her tempted look and lack of immediate refusal had fired his imagination. It had been disappointing, but not wholly unexpected, when she had balked once in his room, so he'd given it one last shot by groveling, not expecting it to work.

Not wanting to waste another minute, he toed off his shoes and stripped his socks off then pushed his pants down, kicking them aside. That left him in his plain, white jock, and he paused, arrested by the blatant admiration in Teri's eyes.

He knew he was in good shape, but his body's appearance became more important to him now as she devoured his form with her hungry gaze. Knowing she watched every movement, he palmed his aching cock over the jock, giving it some much needed counter-pressure.

Her pink tongue snuck out and ran over her lips, leaving a shine he wanted to kiss away. Aaron cocked a brow at her. "Okay, pants are off. What now?"

Teri smiled sensuously and toed off her sandals, giving a sexy shimmy as she slid her shorts down her tanned legs, leaving her in only a pair of simple white panties. "Turn around," she ordered.

Aaron hated to look away, but complied, slowly turning.

"Stop."

He halted his movement and sensed Teri step up close behind him. A bit of movement, then a pair of panties went sailing past him toward his bed. Before he could turn back around, she grasped him by the hips and slid her fingers under the thick elastic of the jock's waistband.

Alternating side-to-side, she slowly pushed the elastic down until it was caught on his almost painfully erect cock. He held his breath, bracing for the coming discomfort but not wanting to interrupt the moment. As if realizing his dilemma, she reached around and took his cock in a tantalizingly brief grip, just long enough to clear the waistband, as she pulled the garment down to the tops of his thighs.

Aaron could sense her kneel down behind him and fought a burst of lust at the mental picture of Teri, nude and on her knees. She finished pulling his jock down to his ankles and let him step out. Then, instead of standing back up, she began stroking down his thighs and he felt her give a gentle bite to his ass cheek.

"Ahh." His head dropped back and his dick gave a heart-stopping jerk as he fought to keep from coming right then and there. She nibbled around to his hip, continuing her light massage of his legs, while turning him around.

Teri zeroed in on his hipbone and he had to fight to keep from pushing her to the floor and pouncing on her. Watching her head move, just inches from his straining erection but purposely avoiding contact, was driving him crazy. He cupped her head with his hand, forcing back the impulse to move her mouth to where he wanted it, and instead loosened her ponytail band, gently removing it to allow her hair to flow down her bare back.

Just then, she glanced up at him from under her lashes, gave him a smile and…stood.

Damn.

He waited for her lead, trembling a bit with the effort of his restraint.

"I thought we were taking a shower," she reminded him with an evil smile as she turned away to enter the bathroom.

"Oh, you are so gonna get it," he growled, stalking after her, patience at an end.

He reached around her and flipped the shower on, adjusting it to the perfect temperature setting then urging her inside, stepping in close behind her.

They took turns shampooing and rinsing their hair under the spray, sliding slowly past one another to exchange places, then began the fun process of 'washing' one another. Standing so near, Teri seemed so small. Her confidence, maturity and presence tended to make him forget how tiny she was.

"You're such a cute little thing," he teased as they soaped up, loving her reaction as he got the arched brow. "How do you do that with just one eyebrow?"

"It's a gift. And I'm *not* a 'cute little thing'. Hardly," she scoffed, tossing her head. "You're just big." She grabbed his erection in a soapy hand, and he almost broke a sweat. "Mmm, and wide too."

"Ah, Teri, the things you say." He loved her playful sexiness. Hell, he loved everything about her. How lucky was he to have her come knocking on his door at such a crappy time in his life?

He pulled her against him, feeling their slick bodies come together, and dipped his head to take her mouth in a lush kiss she returned in full measure.

"God, I just want to pick you up and nail you right against the wall," he muttered as he spread his legs to fit them together even tighter.

"Why don't you?" she invited huskily, and for a brief, wonderful moment, he couldn't think of a single reason why not.

The water pressure suddenly strengthened, and reason came flooding back with it. They looked at each other regretfully, but when Aaron would have turned off the water to get out, she stopped him. "Wait."

Once again, he was treated to the sight of Teri on her knees, but this time the teasing playfulness was gone, replaced by a woman on a mission. He tried to protest, pull her back to her feet, but she refused to budge. She cupped his ball sac in one gentle hand as the other fisted the base of his cock and gave a pump as she wrapped her lips around the head, taking him into that heavenly wet heat.

Aaron dropped back against the wall with a thud and spread his legs even more. Teri flicked her tongue repeatedly just under the head then ran it around the ridge in each direction before slipping her lips down his shaft to where they met her hand. The visual was proving too much, and he could feel the tension building at the base of his spine.

She looked up at him, her eyes smiling as she repeatedly took his cock as far down as her encircling hand, then provided exquisite suction on the way back up, bringing him to the edge of control. He teetered there for a few moments before her finger slipped back and firmly stroked his perineum. That new sensation overwhelmed his efforts to hold back, and he crossed his arms to keep from grabbing her head to hold her in place.

"I'm there, babe," he warned hoarsely, but she didn't pull away, giving one more of those breathtaking strokes behind his balls then he was coming and there was no place to escape from her attention. The very thought that she hadn't pulled back, that she had taken what he had to give, sent an extra, hard pulse through his cock. She gently milked him until the sensation was too much, then finally let him pull her to her feet and up against him.

"I'm sorry."

He got the eyebrow from her again. "I'm not. C'mon. Let's go have dinner."

"What? What about you?" Aaron protested, feeling guilty for having been on the receiving end without giving her pleasure as well.

Teri just laughed. "Don't worry. I wanted to do that. I enjoyed it too. And you can make it up to me later tonight." She got out of the shower and dried off before wrapping up in a bath sheet for the trip to Emery's room.

"Tonight—definitely," Aaron promised, already anticipating the next time in her arms. He couldn't wait to spend the night holding her...

He stopped short as he realized the unexpected direction his thoughts were taking. She wasn't even from here, only visiting for a couple of days, not to mention he wouldn't be around for much longer before he rejoined his team. So even if they did hit it off, where could it go?

Problem was, his brain knew that, but his body already felt the tug of separation as she slipped out of his room to sneak down the hall.

What the hell was he going to do when she went home?

Chapter Eight

Dinner with the Sanduskys had been fun...and not. Teri had laid the foundation for a quick but wholesome meal, and Aaron enjoyed eating well without having to put the time into food prep after a full day of practice. The only thing he'd had to do was grill the steaks, and that was always more of a pleasure than a chore.

He and Teri had found a lot to chat about, mostly about the prospects in spring training camp so far. She was an incredibly knowledgeable fan and Aaron couldn't remember the last time he'd had such an enjoyable, in-depth conversation about his sport with anyone, much less a woman he was interested in.

But sulking off to the side like a dark cloud, all through the prep, meal and cleanup, was her broody son. Aaron rolled his eyes mentally as Emery shrugged off yet another question. Was this what it was like being a parent? Emery wasn't talking, and Teri let him be—for the most part. But Aaron knew there was a talking-to coming and tried to escape, only to be caught as he excused himself for a walk.

"Nope. You're doing this too."

"Why me?" Aaron was honestly puzzled by her desire for his participation. Unless, maybe she needed support?

"I don't see why Aaron needs to enjoy one of your wonderful lectures." Emery finally spoke and his sarcasm immediately got Aaron's back up. "It's not like he's my dad or anything."

And they're off.

Aaron watched Teri take a deep breath, expecting her to cut her son down to size. She was sitting next to Em on the couch, and the young man's body language was definitely hostile. He braced himself for a cold scolding like the kind his own mother would have dished out, his chest tightening in anticipation.

"Can you tell me how your practice went today?"

Aaron let out a breath he hadn't been aware he'd been holding. While Teri's eyes were focused intently on Emery, her expression was far from irritated and her voice was calm.

He wasn't the only one caught off guard by her tactic. The calm tone and non-confrontational interest in his day seemed to surprise Emery and finally earned Teri a look in the eyes from her son. She looked steadily back at him, her love and pride shining through, plain to see. Aaron wasn't even on the receiving end of that look and he was almost choked up. Aaron watched as Emery swallowed convulsively, throat working as he tried to maintain his poise.

"Ma..." Emery's voice broke. "Ah shit, Ma, I'm so sorry." He made as if to reach for her, but she — deliberately it seemed — maintained her distance, not encouraging contact even as she waited for an answer to her question. Aaron could almost see the need in Emery to get a hug and reassurance from his mom.

Emery gathered himself and continued. "Um, practice. It was good. I mean, I had a good day." He shrugged.

Aaron softened a little bit toward him. Cocky was one thing Emery wasn't, and he had every right to be. "He had a great workout today," Aaron interjected to clarify, both to give Teri more information and to boost Emery a bit. "He more than holds his own – he really stands out."

Teri smiled her thanks at him and Emery colored a bit. Aaron nodded to the other player, giving him the floor back.

"Coach called me into his office after practice, and he, uh, said I was looking really good, but I was on the verge of fucking it all up." Em's jaw clenched as he played with the remote. He looked up at his mom. "I swear, I am done screwing around. I mean it. I'm so stupid. I don't want to mess this up. God, this is what I've always wanted to do, and here it is, sooner than I thought."

Teri pressed her lips together, her eyes shiny.

"Ma" – he knelt down in front of her and grabbed her hands – "you've done so much for me. I won't let you down again. I promise."

Tears were rolling down Teri's cheeks, but she was still smiling at Emery. "I love you, Em. You've never let me down, honey. I'm so proud of you." She reeled him in for the much-awaited hug, stroking her hand over his head, their similar hair blending together as they reconciled.

Aaron's chest was tight and his throat thickened just watching them. Finally, he couldn't take it anymore and headed to the kitchen, thinking about his own parents.

He couldn't ever remember either of them telling him they were proud of him, or even that they loved him. His mom was quiet and reserved, and very religious. She thought that sports led to sinful behavior and refused to come to his games.

His dad took a more pragmatic approach to his career. He had pushed Aaron to be the best from an early age, but nothing Aaron ever did was good enough to please him or earn his praise. It was because of his dad's fears of Aaron missing playing time that he'd put off getting corrective surgery when he was younger, and now look at him.

His dad hadn't called him once since the accident, and until now, Aaron hadn't cared. But confronted with the supportive and involved parenting Teri gave to Emery, Aaron found himself aching for what he'd never had. For that unconditional love. He accepted that he'd never get it from his parents, but now that he'd had a taste of it from Teri, he wanted more…

"Hey there. We're done." Teri poked her head around the corner and looked at him closely. "Are you okay?" She walked in and rested a hand on his lower back, just a gentle touch, but it was so like her to always have that hands-on connection.

"It's nothing. I'll be fine." He pulled her into a hug, marveling at how natural, how *right* she felt in his arms. He gave her a peck on top of her head. "How about you?"

"Time will tell. I really think having the coach come down on him helped open his eyes. So in a way, it was good that this all happened sooner rather than later." She gave a little shrug. "I believe *he* believes he's ready to change. He just has to avoid falling back into old habits." Heaving a cleansing sigh, she pulled away, and he reluctantly let her go. "That'll be the hard part. Especially when I'm not here as a reminder."

Aaron nodded, vowing to do what he could to keep an eye on Emery after Teri left, to remind him of his promise to behave and focus.

Teri raised an eyebrow at him. "I know what you're thinking."

"Oh really?" he teased back.

"Yep. And he has to do this on his own. He's not your responsibility."

All of that was true. "Trust me—I know better than anyone that you have to find the drive in yourself in order to succeed in this. It's like anything else. He'll have to do it for himself, not to please you or Coach or me." He shifted to rest back against the edge of the counter. "But it wouldn't hurt him to get a nudge here and there if I can see him slipping. While I'm here, anyway," he amended.

"That's really nice of you. Thank you. I just don't want you stressing about it. You have enough on your own plate." Her gaze went to his shoulder and he rotated it self-consciously, pleased when it didn't give much of a twinge at all.

"Don't worry about me. I don't do anything that I don't want to. I'm a big boy."

Her smile took on a more sensuous cast at his last words, but before he could react, some rather loud music came on out in the living room. They smiled at each other.

"He's making himself at home," Teri observed unnecessarily. "Sorry about that."

"Nah, it's okay. I tend to listen to a lot of music when I'm by myself." He hadn't lately just because it seemed sort of rude to subject other people to what he felt like listening to without checking if it was okay. Better to just avoid the whole topic, though he had to admit that it had seemed unnaturally quiet.

They walked back into the other room to discover that Emery wasn't even in there. No wonder it was loud. He was evidently listening to the music from his bedroom.

Teri headed over to where Emery's phone was plugged into the Bose speaker system.

"Don't worry about it. Why don't we go for a walk before it gets dark? There's a nice trail system that runs along the river and you can get down there a couple of blocks from here. It's really nice and quiet back there—just a few dog walkers and the occasional jogger."

"Is that where you go running?" Teri asked as she reversed direction and went to the front door.

"Yes, sometimes. That trail leads to a park, then you can actually get to a couple of other parks on trails leading from there—all interconnected."

"That sounds really nice. I'd love to. I actually walk every morning. Well," she continued wryly as she sat right down on the floor and grabbed her shoes, "except for this morning, of course. I was sleeping hard and then wham, had to go into action as Supermom and get Em his stuff." She finished lacing up her cross trainers and looked at Aaron expectantly.

He'd been sort of zoning out on her legs and snapped himself back to attention.

Shoes. Right.

Teri smirked at him. "Lost ya there for a sec."

"Oh, no. I was definitely paying attention to you," he retorted and watched a blush creep up from her neck to her cheeks as she rose to her feet.

After he'd donned his own shoes, he glanced back toward the hallway to the bedrooms then looked at Teri. "Should we let him know where we're going?" As soon as he asked, he shook his head just as she did the same.

"He's an adult. And housebroken, for the most part." Teri winked and led the way out of the front door. Aaron went ahead and locked up behind them from habit, then they started down the stairs.

One of the reasons he'd loved the condo complex and had decided to buy there rather than just rent somewhere else was the little park in the back. It used to be a municipal park, but when the developers had purchased the land for the complex, there had been a dispute over access. Eventually the city had sold the developers the park with the caveat that there be public access and right of way. The complex maintained the tiny riverfront park, which tended to flood in the late spring, though it hadn't yet this year. The bonus for the people who lived there was that there was a quiet greenway buffer behind the condos — all you could see was the park and the trees along the river, no other structures or roads.

Another plus was the unofficial dirt path between their small park and the real, city-maintained trail along the river. Enough people cut through there that it was well-defined and only really got overgrown toward the end of summer when all the vegetation was at its peak.

Aaron led her through the trees the short distance to the actual trail, then turned and, on a whim, held out his hand.

Chapter Nine

Teri looked from Aaron's outstretched palm to his face, a bit surprised by the romantic gesture. But that didn't stop her from immediately placing her hand in his as she stepped over the last bit of growth onto the asphalt. He twined his fingers with hers and they began to walk side by side along the river.

At the pace they were going, this didn't have any pretense of being exercise, and it had been ages since she'd just strolled with someone, especially a man. She was used to being in high gear, so it was a novel experience soaking in the stillness of the impending evening while the water moved along beside them. The sound of birds and the distant hum of cars on a road a ways off were the only things breaking the quiet, and they didn't detract from it.

It was nice.

Teri began to consider that she'd missed out on some things in life without even being aware of them. She wouldn't change her circumstance for the world, because that would mean wishing away her two boys, who she loved more than anything, but it was true that it had been an unconventional young adulthood for her. She was used to being in charge...and being alone.

"Penny for them?" Aaron asked. "Or are you just enjoying the walk, I hope?" He accompanied his question with a squeeze of her hand.

"Nothing important. Just thinking about whether I've ever just gone for a walk like this before," Teri admitted.

Aaron looked down at her in surprise. "Well, if you haven't, I'm doubly glad I suggested it then."

"Me too. Sometimes you don't realize you're missing something until something big shakes up your routine."

"Like having your extremely talented son get his shot at the pros?"

"Yep." Teri couldn't keep the proud smile from her face. "Kind of crazy how quickly it all happened."

"It's lucky that you have a flexible job."

Teri smiled wryly. "No luck about it. I put in my time over the years for exactly that reason—so that now I have freedom and I'm not locked in by having to punch a clock."

They walked a bit farther and came to a place on the walkway where they had an unobstructed view of the river. Aaron brought them to a stop and slid his arm around her shoulders as they watched the water go by. A few ducks were floating along, occasionally ducking under with their tails up the air, making Teri smile.

After they resumed their progress, Aaron asked her, "What do you like to do for fun?"

She raised her eyebrow. "Besides watch baseball? What else is there?"

They both laughed.

"I work, work out and watch sports. That's pretty much it," she admitted. "I should probably get a life."

"Hey, that's more than a lot of people do," Aaron protested. "Any other favorite sports...besides the obvious?"

"I do play tennis and golf sometimes wi—" Teri stopped speaking as Aaron's phone began to ring with a twangy country song.

Crap. Aaron let go of her hand as he fumbled in his pocket for it. "Sorry."

"It's okay—go ahead and answer it."

Aaron finally managed to retrieve the phone and hit answer. "*Thanks*" he mouthed to her before answering aloud, "Hey, man, what's up?"

"Holy fucking crap it's a girl, what the fuck am I gonna do man?" All of the words came tumbling out in a rush, and the high pitch to Deke's voice perfectly illustrated his panic. In fact, if he hadn't known it was his friend from the ringtone, he wouldn't have recognized his voice.

"Congrats, Deke."

"No penis!"

He burst out laughing, unable to respond to that right away.

"I'm serious. What the hell? I dunno why, but I really thought it was gonna be a boy."

Teri must have been able to hear Deke's end of the conversation because she offered, "Tell him that sometimes they like to hide their boy parts. Only way to tell for sure is a chromosome test."

Aaron dutifully repeated her words to Deke.

"Naw. Julia ain't goin' for that. You know what they have to do for that? Stick a big ole needle in there! That's fucked up—what if they poke the baby? No fucking way they're..." Deke paused. "Wait...who's that?"

Aaron smiled at Teri. "That's Teri."

"Teri who?"

"Sandusky."

"Sandusky? Huh. Ain't your hotshot a bit young to be married?"

"I'm the hotshot's mom," Teri called out.

"Well hell, man. You don't have me on speaker phone, do ya?" Deke grumbled. "I hate when you do that shit."

Aaron shifted the phone to left hand and held the right back out to Teri, who accepted it. They resumed walking down the path. "I'm always telling you, you have a voice like a foghorn. You aren't on speaker. You're just fucking loud."

"Bite me."

Teri giggled, a light, girlish sound that made Aaron do a pleased double-take, so different was it than her usual low tone of voice.

"Hey, while I got ya, why don't you put the hotshot on? I have some words of wisdom for him, one third-baseman to another."

Aaron would have known better than that even if Emery had been there. Deke just wanted to lecture him on not fucking around or giving Aaron a hard time. "No can do. Teri and I are out on a walk. He's back at the condo."

Silence from the other end of the line.

"You there, Deke?"

"Moonlight stroll? You're hot for Mom?" His answer was almost a whisper—for him. He obviously didn't want to risk Teri overhearing. "Dude, you'd better call me tomorrow. I gotta hear this."

Aaron ignored that. "Tell Julia congratulations and give her big hug from me."

"Ahh...get your ass back here and give her your own damn hug."

He was used to Deke's bluster and knew Julia would be getting his message as soon as they were off the phone, if she wasn't right there on his lap listening in anyway. Deke was crazy in love with his wife and didn't let her get too far away when he wasn't on the road.

"Fine. Will do. G'night."

"Night."

Aaron hung up and pocketed his phone. "Sorry for the interruption."

"No problem. Friend of yours from the team?" she mused. "Deke...southern accent...third baseman... Must be Deacon Rawlson."

Aaron was impressed. "Wow, great job. You do know your baseball, don't you?" He nodded. "Yeah, Deke's probably my best friend."

"You two played together in college too, right?"

"Just for a year before I got called up, but yeah. He went into another team's system, but we stayed in touch, then a couple of trades later, we're in the same place again. It happens that way. You can be bitter rivals then get traded and suddenly become teammates with the enemy, or vice versa. At the same time, it doesn't pay to get super close to anyone because you never know when it'll be over, either because of a trade or injury." He shrugged. "Deke sticks like a freaking burr, though. I have to give him credit. Julia jokes that Deke can't go to sleep at night if he hasn't at least said hi to me once that day. The 'bromance', you know."

He wasn't joking either. The media had picked up on their close friendship, especially when they'd been on rival teams, and rumors still flew even now and then that they were boyfriends. Didn't seem to matter that Deke was married to Julia and now expecting a baby, or that Aaron dated women.

"Well, I'm pretty convinced that the 'bromance' is all in their imaginations. You seem pretty into females to me."

"I'm into you," he corrected and came to a halt to take her in his arms.

That came out a bit more blunt than he'd wanted, but before he could backpedal, Teri rose up to press a kiss to his mouth, murmuring against his lips, "I'd love to really have you 'into' me."

He groaned into her mouth at the sexy invitation, but he was fully aware of their public surroundings, though it had been a while since they'd passed anyone. He kept the kiss mostly chaste, then with a parting peck regretfully pulled back. "Want to head back?"

"Yes, we should probably see if Emery's still there. I'd like to spend some time with him if he is."

"And if he isn't?"

"Then I'll have to settle for an evening in with you." Her eyes promised good things, and Aaron was torn between wishing the condo was empty when they got there, and hoping Em had seen the error of his ways and would be able to hang out with his mom before she left.

The mental reminder of her short time there was definitely a buzzkill and there was quiet between them as they headed back to the path to the condos.

Chapter Ten

Surprisingly enough, Emery was waiting in the living room when they walked in the door. The music still blared.

"Hey, Ma, where'd you go?" Emery looked a bit put out. He was in his comfy, at-home attire—sweats, a T-shirt that she thought she'd used for a rag at least once, and bare feet. While she was happy that he obviously wasn't planning to go repeat last night's mistake, part of Teri would have enjoyed putting an empty condo to good use again.

"Aaron and I went for a walk." She crossed the room to plop down next to him on the couch. "He showed me a nice path along the river."

Aaron grabbed a remote and used it to lower the volume of the music then went into the kitchen.

"Could he even keep up with ya? For a shrimp you sure do walk fast." Emery grinned at her.

She didn't bother telling him about just strolling. He either wouldn't believe her or he'd think it was weird. "I'm not a shrimp," she played her part.

"You're too short to even be a good place to rest my arm anymore." He nudged her.

She smacked his arm. "You need to stop growing then. And stop leaning on me."

"I was going to see if you guys wanted to put a game on, but I don't know. Is it safe to come in?" Aaron appeared with a couple of glasses of iced water. He handed one to Teri then sat in a chair on the opposite side of the room.

"Yeah, that'd be great. And it's just the usual bickering. This one doesn't like to let me forget that he grew taller than me at twelve years old."

Emery snickered when Teri gave him a mock shove then rested against his shoulder. Emery automatically put his arm around her for a hug and they sat that way as they watched Aaron flip through the channels until he found a ball game for them to watch.

It wasn't often that Teri found herself distracted from a game, but her mind and gaze kept wandering to Aaron lounging a short distance away. He glanced over and their eyes met. A current passed between them that Emery was thankfully unaware of. Aaron's heated regard traced her from head to toe and back up again, and she felt that perusal like a physical touch.

At that point, Teri excused herself and headed down the hall to Emery's room. She was woefully out of practice at exchanging covert romantic looks with someone while one of her kids was in the room. She took a deep breath as she double-checked her appearance in the mirror above the dresser.

A knock came at the door. "Teri? You okay?"

Her cheeks instantly pinkened at the sound of Aaron's low voice. "Yes, just a moment." She took a couple of steps to the door then paused to gather herself before she opened it.

Aaron looked her up and down but made no effort to enter. "You all right?"

"Fine, just needed a breather." Now, why had she admitted that?

"Oh yeah?"

He was killing her, lounging there with his broad shoulder leaning against the doorjamb, a slightly smug smile on his face as though he knew exactly why she'd fled the room.

She thought about their shower then flashed back to the uncharacteristic and raunchy comment she'd made out on the path, and couldn't keep her gaze from drifting below his waist. The soft material of his sweats did little to hide the fact that he was just as into this flirtation as she was.

As she watched, he dropped a hand to cup his semi-hard cock. "See what you do to me? Hard to keep from showing it. Makes me interested in what I might be doing to you." Aaron leaned back and glanced down the hall, then stepped inside the room and closed the door.

Teri moved into his arms and he braced his back against the door, which had no lock. She sent a mental plea for Emery to stay interested in the game for at least a few more minutes. His eyes searching hers, Aaron toyed with the elastic waistband of her shorts then delved inside, bypassing her panties and gripping her bare ass. Then he moved one hand around her hip, still inside her clothing, to trace along her pubic hair.

She couldn't keep from licking her lips as he stopped moving, and his gaze dropped to her mouth. She parted her lips, unable to get enough oxygen through her nose, the anticipation driving her crazy. With the warm pulsing between her thighs, she craved his touch on her pussy. Then he surprised her by sliding that hand upward to cup one of her breasts instead.

"Tease," she breathed.

His lips spread in a wicked grin, and he ran a thumb across her beaded nipple. Unexpectedly, he used the hand that had been caressing her ass to reach farther down into her pants, finding the slickness of her pussy from the rear.

She gasped and arched as his finger entered her.

"You are so wet." His thumb teased at her nipple while he pumped slowly in and out of her grasping channel. "God, I could just sink into you."

"Yes." She didn't realize she'd said that aloud until it reached her own ears in the quiet of the room.

His expression regretful, he withdrew his fingers, leaving a slight trail of moisture as he skirted his hand past her ass and out of her pants. The other hand he slid around behind her and pulled her into a hug.

"We can't right now. Later?" he whispered in her ear.

God, he had more willpower than she did. She just wanted to rip his clothes off and have him do her against the wall. If only they were alone...

But they weren't.

She blew out a breath then nodded. "Later. If I can," she added. "It might be really late." Who knew when Em would get to bed? And it obviously wasn't going to happen while he was awake, a fact that she was grateful for Aaron being the one to remember and put on the brakes for.

He nodded, squeezed her one last time then firmly put her away from him before reaching for the doorknob. "You go first. I need to put on something a bit thicker," he muttered, looking down at his obvious erection with chagrin. "Damn thing. I swear I usually have more control than this."

Teri chuckled as she moved past him into the hallway before she succumbed to temptation and jumped him.

Aaron's laughter joined hers as he headed toward his bedroom and she returned to where Emery was still slouched in the living room, eyes glued on the set.

"You didn't miss much," he informed her.

"Good," she responded automatically, settling in next to him again.

But I'm actually missing quite a lot right now.

* * * *

Aaron glanced at the glowing numbers of the bedside clock again and sighed. The Sanduskys had outlasted him. He'd started yawning around midnight, and finally Emery had noticed. "Hey, man, you don't have to stay up just 'cause we are." He'd even turned down the volume, but didn't look the least bit tired. Then he'd resumed chatting with his mom about his impressions of some of the other teams in their division.

Teri had looked at Aaron ruefully and given him a slight shrug. It had been obvious that Emery wasn't going to turn in anytime soon, so he'd gotten up and said his goodnights, then had gone through his nighttime routine and hit the sack.

He might be tired, but he couldn't turn his brain off, not when his thoughts kept returning to Teri. His erection continued to make its presence known as well, but he didn't want to get himself off if there was any chance at all that Teri might join him later.

So here he was, staring at the dark ceiling and listening.

He must have drifted off at some point because the next thing he knew, he felt the dip and movement of the mattress.

"It's me," Teri whispered as a cool draft preceded her touch and the covers settled over the both of them. He shifted to wrap an arm around her and pull her close. She rested a cool hand on his chest and her head on his good shoulder. "He finally went to bed. I thought he'd never wind down."

"Me either. But I'm glad you got some good visiting with him in."

"Me too." Teri moved a bit and he felt her lips touch his pec, her warm breath skating over his skin. "I don't want to talk about him at the moment, though."

"What do you want to talk about?" he teased, running a hand along her back. She must have changed, because there was a softer, thinner feel to whatever top she was wearing. He slid his hand down her side along the dip of her waist and swell of her hip...and reached bare skin. Nothing on the bottom then.

"Maybe I don't want to talk." She lifted her leg to nudge between his and entwine them. He could feel her pussy hair against his flank and thanked heaven he was wearing briefs, otherwise he'd be tempted to pull her on top of him and slide right into her without any protection at all.

Instead, when he *did* pull her on top of him, they had that thin barrier between them as she bent to press her lips to his. She settled her welcome weight on top of his hard cock and wriggled around for a few seconds as their kiss deepened in a hurry. It went from a hello to an all-out carnal mating of mouths in seconds as she rode his cock, rocking along his length while he bracketed her bare hips with his hands and allowed her to set the pace.

He lifted his head slightly to add movement to the kiss, stroking into her accepting mouth with his tongue and kneading her ass as a rhythmic counterpoint to their thrusts. The heat between them was incendiary and it was becoming harder by the moment to remember why he couldn't roll her over, lose the briefs and bury himself in her.

Before he could lose his control, he stilled her hips then pushed her from atop him.

"What's…?" Her protest trailed off as he ran his hands up her torso, taking her sleepshirt up and off. He reluctantly left his underwear in place for the moment then gently guided her onto her back and moved to kneel between her thighs.

Her pale skin glowed in the tiny bit of light coming from between the partially open blinds. He ran his hands along the soft skin of her inner legs then moved downward to trace a trail of kisses up one thigh. Aaron smiled at the sigh of response and gave the other leg the same treatment before going to his belly on the sheets, shoulders between her legs, supporting them slightly. He shifted to adjust his cock to a comfortable angle then kissed his way as teasingly and slowly as he could to her core, wrapping his hands around her upper thighs to hold them in place as she gave an impatient buck.

"Aaron…"

"I'm getting there," he promised.

"Get there faster."

He raised his head to laugh softly and met her eyes in the dimness of the room. "Yes, Teri."

It was almost more than she could handle, having him down there and not doing a damn thing to assuage her ache, an ache that had been hounding her since their walk earlier.

Now that they were in the privacy of Aaron's room, behind a locked door and under the secrecy of darkness, he should be doing something besides laughing at her impatience, damn it...

His mouth unerringly latched onto her clit and she almost yelled with her relief. She clapped a hand over her mouth just in time, then fumbled around to grab a pillow and placed it over her head.

"Hey, now, don't smother yourself."

"Enough talking," she whispered and strained against his iron grip on her lower body. "Or I'll smother you instead."

His huffed laugh fanned warmth over her wet clit, immediately followed by a long, meandering lick from there downward to her moist core.

Teri whacked him on the back with the pillow then sent it winging across the bed as he nibbled and licked his way back to give her peak the attention it craved. With how turned on she'd been all night, it didn't take any time at all before she was on the edge of losing control.

She ran her fingers into his hair, but the short cut didn't allow her to grip easily and it turned into more of a caress. Suddenly, the pressure became almost too much, as though the coming orgasm would be way too intense.

She jerked her head up. "Aaron," she called urgently, trying hard to get him to back off, but he had his own ideas on the matter. He kept right at what was making her crazy. Her head thumped back on the pillows and her body arched as she went supernova against his talented mouth.

He groaned against her then covered her with his body, meeting her mouth in a wet kiss that tasted of him combined with her own slick juices. His rigid erection settled right against her pussy and she realized he hadn't even taken off his briefs yet.

Her hands went to his waistband in the back and she began to tug at them, trying to get them off. "Off, off," she chanted. "C'mon. I want skin."

"Too tempting, unless I immediately put on a condom," he warned, still thrusting against her. The drag of the fabric against her sensitized clit was promising, but at the same time, she needed more. She needed to be filled.

"Do it then. I want you in me. Been wanting it since our walk. Since we met," she babbled. She continued yanking until she feared she would rip the underwear right in two.

"Fuck, you're hot." Finally, Aaron got with the program and knelt up, but only pushed his briefs down enough to expose his cock and balls before taking his cock into a firm grip. "Can't wait this time. Tomorrow," he promised huskily as he pumped himself, obviously right on the edge.

She reached down to cup his balls in her hands and almost immediately he began to come. Teri lightly massaged his balls and cupped her other hand above his under the head of his cock, forming a curve for him to thrust into, come into.

Aaron threw his head back. "Fuck, Teri," he growled before pinning her with his gaze. "You're killing me. God." He slid his cock along her cum-filled palm a few more times, then she took over, stroking his cum down his still-firm shaft, mindful that it was probably very sensitive. After a few passes, he gripped her by the wrist and she let go. Only then did he take off his briefs and offer them to her as a rag.

She wiped off her hand then he took it and swabbed at himself a few times before tossing them out of view and taking her into his arms. They settled together and Aaron reached to pull the covers up from somewhere.

"I can't fall asleep in here," she murmured even as she snuggled in against his strong chest, enjoying the warmth and closeness.

"Sure you can. We'll be up before him."

"But what if he gets up in the middle of the night and notices—?"

"Teri..." Aaron cut her off.

She stilled, listening.

"Would it be the end of the world if by chance he learned that something had happened between us?"

Teri thought about that for a minute. Would it be? The answer was no. Em and Alex were adults now, and she was more than just a mom. In fact, Alex had been after her for years to start dating. He'd likely be thrilled. But Emery was a bit oblivious to the fact that she had a life beyond work and parenting. Not that she actually had much of one.

"I guess not. Still, it isn't exactly the way I'd want to broach the subject."

Aaron nodded. "Fair enough. Stay for a little while? Then you can move back out to the couch if you're more comfortable with that. I don't want you to do anything that will detract from what's happening between us."

Silence reigned at that point, and she really tried to just enjoy the time for what it was. But Aaron's choice of words kept circling in her head and continued to do so long after she eased away from Aaron's sleeping form and made her way back out to the cold sofa.

What exactly is *happening between us?*

Chapter Eleven

When Aaron woke up and Teri was gone from his bed, he wasn't surprised—just even more determined to convince her to stay with him tonight. Nothing she'd said suggested that she had done much dating, so between work and raising Emery, he figured she was due for some adult fun. That much he could deliver on.

A huge part of him wished, however, that he'd met her at home, not here. Something about Teri really seemed to click with him, and for the first time, he could really see getting involved with someone being worth it…if she had lived in the same city, that was.

He knew better than to get his hopes up for a future with her under the circumstances. It was hard enough on players' partners with all of the travel…he couldn't imagine lumping a long distance relationship on top of that. They'd never see one another.

Stretching, he tried to convince himself to get up, and finally was able to do so when he remembered that he might be able to have some one on one time with Teri if Emery slept as late as he typically seemed to. They had a while before they had to be at the stadium.

Once he was cleaned up and dressed, Aaron left his room and quietly made his way into the living room. He needn't have bothered. Teri was awake, dressed and on the phone.

"…probably tomorrow then, hon. I'd like to stay one more day to make sure that he's settled in. He's doing pretty well, though. I'm hopeful this will work out." She listened for a minute then grinned. "Most likely. I'm just deluding myself that he'll behave when I'm not here, aren't I? But we did have a good talk last night. Before that I was trying hard not to feel like the worst parent in the world." Teri's expression had sobered and she sighed.

Aaron took a few steps toward her, wanting to comfort her. That brought her attention to him. She smiled and held up a finger indicating she would be a minute. He nodded and headed toward the kitchen.

Before he left the room, he heard her say, "Thanks. I can always count on you. And thanks for passing on the message, hon. I know. Love you too. See you tomorrow. Oh, that reminds me…" She trailed off as though the other person had started speaking.

Aaron stopped short. Who the hell was she talking to that she loved and called 'hon'? He shook his head and resumed walking. Probably just a close girlfriend. Teri wasn't the type who would mess around if she was involved with someone. And no way was Aaron going to ask. Though, if she happened to mention who she'd been talking to, he wouldn't mind that at all.

He noticed that Teri had made a pot of coffee. He didn't always drink it but liked the taste with certain breakfasts, so he went ahead and fixed a mug for himself. He was up early enough, and with company here, maybe he'd go ahead and cook something.

He hadn't noticed whether Teri had coffee yet or not, so he walked back into the living room to check and to offer her some if she hadn't got it already.

Yeah, right. You just want to hear more of her conversation with 'hon'.

But she was already off the phone and coming toward him with a distracted expression that changed into a smile for him. "Hey there. I made coffee, but wasn't sure what you might want to eat."

"Good morning," he finally said and took her into his arms for a hug. When had she starting fitting against him so perfectly? A bit freaked out, Aaron dropped his arms. "You don't have to cook every meal while you're here. Believe me, I fed myself long before you came along." He had meant for that to sound teasing, but it came out a bit more sarcastic than humorous. He tried again, "I just mean that you're my guest while you're staying here. It's my kitchen. I should be the one making you breakfast." He wasn't sure that sounded any better. Man, he was making a mess of things this morning. Truth be told, he was a bit off kilter between overhearing the conversation with someone important in her life and the sure knowledge that Teri would be leaving tomorrow, all juxtaposed against his growing comfort and attraction around her.

Her smile had faded and she looked a bit puzzled. Probably trying to figure out what his problem was.

"Sorry," he apologized. "Not sure why everything's coming out wrong this morning." He moved closer and touched her forearm. "I had a great night, so it's not that."

She seemed reassured by that if the returning smile was any indication, but before they could say anything further, Emery stumbled down the hall, surprising them both into stepping back from each other.

"Wow. You're up early, honey." Teri reached up and gave his hair a ruffle as he staggered by them into the kitchen. After exchanging an amused glance, Aaron and Teri followed him in.

"Yeah, well, *someone* texted me, like, *ten* times this morning telling me to get my ass out of bed and spend some time with you 'cause you have to go home tomorrow 'cause of something for work," Emery groused as he poured himself some coffee.

Teri smirked. "Sorry about that."

"No you're not. Just 'cause you guys are freakish morning people doesn't mean we all are. Not that I don't want to spend time with you or anything. He's just a bossy fucker who needs to get a life. He has no right to—"

"Watch your language, Emery."

"He *is* bossy." Emery snickered into his mug.

Teri sighed. "Not the word I have a problem with. So"—she clapped her hands together and her son winced—"you're up. What do you want for breakfast? Aaron and I were just talking about that."

That got Emery's attention. "Why don't we go out? My treat."

Teri immediately got a suspicious look on her face. "What?"

"Your treat, huh?" Teri pinned Emery with a look.

"Jeez, can't a guy take his mom out to breakfast without her getting all conspiracy theory on his ass?"

Aaron sipped his coffee, enjoying the twosome's banter, but unbelievably curious about who Teri had been talking to, who was also a man and knew her son well enough to text him and wake him up. The dad missing from the picture?

"Hmm, well, there was that one time where you 'accidently borrowed' and used someone else's credit card to take me to dinner."

"That *was* an accident!" Emery protested

"You accidently had his ID too. Then there was the time you took me out for brunch at that expensive place with the waiting list for reservations but forgot your wallet so I had to buy."

He huffed and crossed his arms. "I changed pants at the last minute. Man, you remember everything."

"How about the time you picked the perfect place for Mother's Day…because of the hot waitress you wanted to — ?"

"Ma!" Em interrupted, pointing at Aaron. "Come on! He doesn't want to hear about all of that. I'm sure he just wants to eat some great pancakes at this place I heard about — The Ginger Cat."

Aaron had to nod. "They do have great pancakes. And they're pretty reasonably priced, from what I remember."

"See?" Em pouted slightly. "I just wanted to make it up to you for yesterday. Sheesh. And, well, I heard it's a good all-you-can-eat special on the pancakes today," he mumbled against the coffee mug before taking a long drink and polishing it off and grimacing like it was medicine.

Teri walked up to give Emery a hard hug as soon as he finished. "Thanks, hon. I'd love to have you take me out for pancakes. Why don't you go get ready?" She patted him on the back, and he headed out of the kitchen and down the hall much more quickly than he'd come.

Aaron made to follow him so he could get socks and shoes, but Teri surprised him by sliding her arms around his waist as he went to pass her.

"I never got a proper good morning," she murmured.

"I won't mention that you would have gotten a very proper good morning if you'd stayed with me last night and woken up beside me."

"Oh, you're not going to mention that, are you? Good to know."

Aaron smiled and gave her a quick kiss. "Maybe we could try it that way tonight."

"Me staying all night? Or something else?"

"Well, I seem to recall that you might have wanted something last night that I didn't get a chance to deliver."

"Mmm," Teri agreed. "Tonight might be a good time for that. Especially since...well..." She sighed, dropping the teasing act. "I have to head home. A job I'd planned to start next week just got complicated and they need me there yesterday. Surveyors showed up earlier than they expected. Nothing they can do about it now, but I need to be there to start damage control for the expected survey results so they can get their action plan together. And...this is way more than you needed to know," she apologized. "Sorry. Slipped right into work mode there for a minute." She shrugged. "Kind of on my mind now. I'd told them they should have me in there sooner than this. Ah well."

It had been a fascinating glimpse into a part of herself he hadn't seen before, so he didn't mind. "You'll have to tell me more about your job at breakfast."

"Em will love that." She rolled her eyes. "But I can talk fast while he's cramming pancakes into his mouth."

They shared a laugh then one more pecked kiss before they both headed down the hall to get ready. Aaron couldn't do anything about the fact that practice would take up much of their last day together, but he was planning on making the most of this morning...and tonight.

* * * *

Teri rubbed the base of her back and rotated her head. Fairly satisfied that she'd be prepared to go in to the facility being surveyed the day after tomorrow ready to get to work, she closed down her laptop and stowed it in its case, along with the cord. She was done with work until she got home, and besides, the guys would be back from practice soon.

She'd put together a simple enough meal of a vegetable frittata — already cooked and cooling — and a tossed garden salad, then had gone ahead and baked a peach and blackberry cobbler for dessert. All of the menu filling and satisfying to eat, but simple to make from what they'd had on hand.

Teri sighed. There really wasn't much more for her to do here, and no good reason she couldn't have driven home today. Emery seemed settled and in a positive frame of mind, and Aaron was a great role model for him. She could be at home tonight, preparing for work there.

But that would mean missing another night in Aaron's arms, and she wasn't ready for that to be over. Not yet.

The front door opened as though her thoughts had conjured him up, and first Aaron then Emery stepped in. Her automatic smile got caught somewhere between a mom greeting for her son and appreciation of the man she'd been fortunate enough to explore — and be explored by — over the past couple of days.

She coughed and turned away.

"Hey, Ma. Glad you're still here." Emery gave her a brief side hug as he strode past.

"What do you mean?"

He paused before going down the hallway, obviously intent on a shower. "Well, I sort of figured with the work thing and all you might have headed home today. Everything's cool here. No reason to stay...not that I'm rushing you off or anything," he clarified hurriedly. "I like having you here."

"I understand, honey. I had considered it, but" — Teri looked at Aaron who was absorbing the whole conversation with a slight frown — "I...like being here too."

"Alex was just surprised you didn't get on the road today. He blames me, I think. Like you have to babysit me or something." Emery's trademark frustration with Alex was evident on his face. Honestly, it would piss her off sometimes if she didn't know that Emery would be the first to heatedly defend Alex against anyone else.

"That's not it at all. I'll talk to him," she soothed and flapped her hands at him. "Go — shower. Dinner's ready anytime."

"Awesome!" He disappeared down the hall and less than ten seconds later the shower could be heard.

Teri turned to face Aaron. "Hey there."

"Hi."

The flat greeting was a bit out of character, but she didn't know him well enough to call him on it, so she proceeded as though she hadn't noticed a difference. "Good to see you. Um, I made dinner."

"Thanks, but I told you you didn't have to do that."

Teri began to get irritated by the abrupt change. "I know I didn't have to, but I wanted to. I thought it would be nice to have dinner in tonight. Plus I enjoy cooking for more than just myself. I sort of miss it now that I'm an empty nester."

"So you don't cook for Alex?"

She frowned. "Well, sometimes, maybe a couple of times a week usually, but our schedules don't always coincide, especially this time of year. It's been a while."

"Is Alex another ballplayer then?"

It might have been her imagination, but that came across with almost a sneer. She had to smile a bit, though, since the thought of Alex playing baseball was beyond humorous. The boys couldn't be more different in that respect.

"No, he's doing tax—"

Aaron cut her off, "Accountant. Smart guy instead of a dumb jock. I get it. No need to continue."

The interruption was the last straw. "What the hell is your problem?" she demanded. "How could you think that *I* of all people think jocks are dumb? Is your blood sugar low? Or are you always just an asshole after practice?"

"How am I being an asshole? Because I don't want to hear you go on about Alex doing taxes?" The very reasonable tone of his voice was negated by the glare he sent her way.

"I can't believe this! Now you're yelling at me for answering a simple question? I can't believe I stayed here for you!"

"I never asked you to. And I'm not the one raising my voice."

She pressed her lips together. That *had* come out a bit loudly, and the last thing she wanted was for Emery to hear her screeching at Aaron...even if he deserved it a bit.

Teri tried to put herself in Aaron's shoes. Maybe she'd been a mom too long. She didn't think she was like some parents who went on and on about their kids' accomplishments, but it might seem that way to a young man who'd never had children. She swallowed her anger and tried to take the high road, even though what he'd said about not asking her to stay stung.

"My apologies for yelling. You're right—you never raised your voice. But obviously something has you upset with me, and I think I know what it is. I just want to get along until I go tomorrow, so I'll watch what I say. Okay?"

Aaron couldn't believe how sideways the conversation had gone, but he'd be damned if he'd sit there and watch Teri go all soft in the eyes about another man—someone who was there in her real life, someone she'd be returning to tomorrow.

It made him a bit queasy to consider how quickly he'd grown attached to Teri.

Stupid.

Stupid to feel jealous after such a short time and no words about the future, and stupid to still be standing there, sweaty and dirty from practice while he made things worse with his stupid mouth.

He'd never been very good at arguing. To say that his parents' relationship was dysfunctional was an understatement. His father dictated, and his mother kowtowed. No deviation was permitted.

Aaron swallowed as he considered that perhaps he was trying to fit himself and Teri into that box. He wouldn't do that, would he? Not knowingly, but who knew? It wasn't like he knew what a real relationship was like.

Speaking of relationships, he had no right to know anything about what hers was with Alex. But having seen her face when he came up and overhearing her conversation with him earlier, it was obvious that she at least cared strongly for him. Maybe they weren't committed enough to keep her from feeling free to mess around with Aaron...or maybe he just had her pegged wrong.

His silence must have stretched on too long because she was staring at him with an expectant frown. He might as well get out of their hair and go for a walk. He took a step back toward the door, but she quickly came forward and caught his arm. "I need to head home tomorrow." She looked up at him solemnly, regretfully. "I'm not sure if I'll be back before you go back to your team."

"I figured." Aaron didn't know what to say. She had her own life, and he was only here temporarily anyway. Pretty soon, after spring training wound down and the teams were set, Aaron would go home, rejoin his own team and fight to get back into playing condition.

He watched as she obviously struggled to put something into words, and he had a feeling what it was. He tried to help her out. "What we said this morning about getting together tonight? It's... Well, maybe it's better if — "

"Yeah," she cut him off abruptly, pinkening and looking away. "Thanks for making this easier. After all, it was just a...fling."

A shaft of hurt speared through him, to have their time together reduced to a fling. How ironic to be on the receiving end of the 'we were just having a good time' line now that he really felt a connection. She was already looking for the easy way out, to leave with a clear conscience? Fine with him.

"I really just want to take a walk." He glanced down at where she still had hold of his forearm and she removed her grip quickly.

He headed toward the door again, and this time, she let him go.

Chapter Twelve

"Okay, son, tell Papa Deke what ails ya."

Aaron smiled half-heartedly. "It's all good. What's up with you? How's Julia and the baby?"

"Quit tryin' to distract me. You've been way too quiet. You need to fuckin' tell me if you've got bad news about your arm."

Aaron's eyebrows went up at the very serious tone to Deke's voice. "No, nothing like that. It's actually improving, and they're happy with my progress."

"Well, shit, then it must be girl trouble. And ain't no cure for a broken heart."

"My heart's not broken." *Just a little bruised.* "Where did you get that idea? There's no one down here I'm interested in." Which was the truth. Hadn't been for two weeks.

"Uh-huh."

"Seriously."

"You only ever try to convince me of how serious it is when you're protesting overmuch, as Will Shakespeare would say. Now come clean before I have to come down there and clean your clock," he threatened with a growl.

Deke would no more lay a hand on him than on Julia. Fuck, what would it hurt to tell him? "Fine. Just to keep you from having to make a trip—and by the way, I'd be more worried about Julia's reaction than you." He paused. "You remember I mentioned Sandusky's mom?"

"Teri, right?"

"Yeah. She…well…" Shit it was hard talking about stuff like this.

"Spit it the fuck out, man. What? You guys hooked up?"

"Sort of." Though he didn't think of it that way. "Not like a hook up, one-nighter or anything. She's not that kind of woman." At least, he didn't think she was, though the whole situation made him question his judgment.

All he knew was that he missed her and wished he'd done so many things differently. Like maybe actually asking her about her relationship status.

"So what kind of woman is she then?"

Aaron found himself spilling almost everything to his friend, who listened silently as he described their connection, the fun they'd had and his worries about the involvement of Alex in her life.

"I don't know if the guy is Emery's dad or a friend or what, but she obviously cares about him and is right there in her life. I don't know." He was pacing back and forth. "I just don't know what to do. I miss her."

He realized he'd been monopolizing the conversation for an age. "Deke?"

"Still here, man, not that it woulda mattered to you. Ya ever thought about just askin' her about the guy? Or, if not her, then askin' the kid?"

Aaron sighed, frustrated. "What, I should just ask him who his mom's involved with?"

"Why not? And you can be less obvious about it than that. C'mon. Man the fuck up and figure this shit out. I'm tired of listenin' to your mopey ass."

That got a laugh out of Aaron, who found he felt better after having spilled his secret to his friend. "Okay. I'll try to do that. Eventually she'll come back to see Emery play. I'm pretty sure he's going to earn a spot on the AAA team, so he'll stay here."

"Well, good for the kid. Glad he got his shit together. Now it's time for you to do the same. Am I right?"

"Amen."

Emery walked into the room, texting or playing a game on his phone.

"Gotta go, man. Thanks for the talk. Kiss Julia for me."

"Kiss her your own damn self, I keep tellin' ya."

Aaron grinned as he said goodbye and hung up. "Hey, Emery, you got a sec?"

Emery jerked his head up, looking surprised, as well he should be. Even though they lived together, it wasn't like they had heart-to-hearts all that often. Or ever.

"Sure," he said warily, but he gamely crossed the room and sat down on the couch. "What's up?"

Aaron felt stupid. *Damn Deke for getting me into this.* Might as well get it over then. "Oh, it just occurred to me that you never mention your dad." There—that was subtle.

Emery's lip curled. "Dave? Why would I? He never wanted anything to do with us in the first place." He shrugged, looking more annoyed than upset. "He lives in Texas now, I think. We don't really talk to him, and I personally don't have a problem with that. Why?"

Well, obviously Dave wasn't the mysterious Alex. Which was...good? He thought.

"Just wondering. I'm not close to my dad either."

That caught Emery's interest a bit. "How about your mom?"

Aaron shook his head.

Emery frowned, seeming perplexed. "Wow. I can't imagine that. Ma's, like, the biggest influence in my life." He studied Aaron for a few moments. "So if you're not close to either of them, who's your family?"

He shrugged. "Don't really consider myself to have an official one, but my best friend Deke and his wife are like family. That was just him on the phone," he added. Before he could chicken out he made himself ask, "So your mom — Teri — she's been single a long time. Does she date?"

His charge's mouth dropped open. "Ma? Date? No, never, at least not that I know of." He sat up straight, a sudden realization clearly hitting him. "Which...is odd, for someone her age and personality. Right? I mean, she should have dated *someone* by now, especially now that... Crap." Emery stood and took a few steps then spun around. "Sorry, is our talk over? I've gotta..." He made a vague gesture with his phone toward his room.

"No problem," Aaron reassured him and Emery took off like a shot, already dialing someone.

Well that had been somewhat informative. Teri obviously wasn't seeing Alex, at least not openly enough to where her son was aware of it. So maybe there was a chance for him...

Yeah, not to rain on your parade, but there's still the living-in-different-cities thing…
Shut up.

* * * *

Teri had no choice but to throw herself into work once she got home. The long days spent on the new client facility, helping them address the issues found during their survey, as well as doing other scheduled visits, kept her mind occupied during waking hours.

But the nights…

Oh, how she regretted things with Aaron, though she fluctuated on the reason. Some nights she wished she'd never started anything with him so her body wouldn't know what it was missing. Other nights she wished she'd stopped that last weird fight and spent that night with Aaron, to hell with her pride. Or spent the prior night with him and woken up beside him in the morning.

Alex wasn't around much because of how busy he was with school and work, and Emery was doing well and staying busy, so she quickly got sick of being alone, longing for someone to talk to. She lost track of how many times she almost dialed the condo's phone number, then changed her mind at the last moment.

Two weeks after she'd gotten home, she got a phone call from Emery.

"Okay, Ma, what's up with you?"

"Hi, honey. What do you mean?" She sat back in her chair after closing down her laptop to focus all of her attention on her son.

"I mean, why the hell haven't you come back here? You're not that busy with work anymore. Did you and Aaron have a fight or something?"

"What?" Her voice went a bit higher than normal with her shock at the perceptive question. She cleared her throat. "Why would you think something like that?"

"Because Alex thought we'd been in a fight 'cause you've been acting weird and down since you got back. And I know that we were fine when you left, so I thought maybe it was Aaron, 'specially since he's been weird and down too."

"And you didn't answer the question, I noticed," Alex unexpectedly chimed in. "Way to throw me under the bus, by the way, Em."

"Hey, I'm just reporting the news. You're the guy who made it."

Teri sighed in exasperation. "I wish you guys would quit three-way calling me without telling me you're both on the line."

"So?" Alex prodded.

"First of all, it's none of your business either way. Second of all, how on earth would you guys even have time to notice if anything was wrong with me? It's not like I've talked to either of you…"

"That's precisely my point," Alex agreed. "You've been very hands-off for the past two weeks—which is exactly how long you've been back from there. So if Emery wasn't the problem…for a change…"

"Hey!"

"…then something else had to have happened. And Aaron was the only other person there."

Teri realized her boys were worried about her, and while that was incredibly sweet, there was no way she was sharing any of the details with her sons. "I'm fine with Emery, and I'm fine with Aaron too. And Alex for that matter. I'm just"—she paused, wanting to be truthful without giving too much away—"working some things out for myself. Mid-life crisis stuff, you know," she joked.

"If you buy a sports car, I get to drive it first," Emery voted.

"Whatever. You already have your over-compensating mega-truck," Alex shot back.

"Says the man with the Volvo. Seriously—who the fuck drives a Volvo besides boring old people?"

"Boys," Teri interjected before the sibling teasing got out of hand. "I'm really flattered that you were worried enough about me to do a conference call, but I'm fine. I just think that both of you—yes, *both*, Alex, and that includes your brother—are old enough to be responsible for yourselves, without your mom hovering over you. That's part of it anyway," she owned up. "And the rest is my business. Okay?"

Silence as the two did whatever mental telepathy twins seemed to be born with.

"Okay, Ma. As long as you're okay, and you don't hate being around us or anything."

That was her pouter, Emery, who was used to being the focus of her attention. He would feel more at loose ends than his brother. She promised herself she'd make time for a private phone call with him soon to reassure him.

"Hardly," she answered. "Love you both to death and you know it."

"Love you too," Emery answered right away. "You're going to come down when I start my first game, right?"

"Of course, hon," she replied. Meanwhile, Alex, her thinker, was being overly quiet. "Alex?" she prodded.

"Yeah, Ma. Love you too."

She made a kissing noise. "All right. You guys go back to whatever it is you do, and I'll talk to each of you soon."

They said a round of goodbyes, and she finally got them both off the phone, then sat back, considering. What she had said was true. It was time to cut the apron strings. And if that meant staying away from Aaron too, maybe a bit of time and perspective would lend clarity to that situation.

By the time she went back to see Emery play, she'd know what to do.

Chapter Thirteen

"Hey, Ma! Are you here? Where are you sitting?"

Aaron had known Teri was coming to this game and couldn't help but listen as Emery walked out of the dugout with his phone, looking up into the stands. He found himself surreptitiously scanning the third-base side of the grandstand along with Emery, using where Em was looking as a guide.

Spotting her even before Emery—how he couldn't see her yet was beyond him—he had to smile at the picture Teri made in her oversized team uniform top. She looked like a kid all dressed up in her big brother's clothing, especially wildly waving her arm over her head like that. God, he'd missed her this past month. He couldn't wait to talk to her again, try to get back to their previous comfort with one another.

Aaron couldn't say why it was so important to him to reconnect with her. He'd only really known her for a couple of days, but he hadn't been able to get her out of his mind since then.

"Oh there you are! Hey! You brought Alex? Oh, man, why didn't you tell me he was coming? No wonder you're staying at a hotel."

Alex? He's here?

"I'm surprised, all right. *Sure* I'm glad to see him." He pulled out the 'sure' sarcastically. "I just hate that you love him more than me."

What the fuck?

"I know, I know, love is like a flame, yada, yada. Hey, I've gotta go. I'll meet you after. Come to the apartment."

No, no.

She apparently argued against that too. "Okay, dinner. How about Seifert's? Go get a table, and I'll get there as soon as I can. Wish me luck. Bye."

Aaron was stunned. Teri had brought Alex here? And she loved him? He went cold. Maybe the guy *had* already been in her life prior to their meeting, even though Emery hadn't known about it. After all, he hadn't known about Teri's brief interlude with Aaron. How long ago did they get together?

He was burning with questions, but wasn't sure how to ask Emery what he needed to know without giving away his interest. Fortunately, Emery was his usual chatty self.

"Can you believe Ma brought that loser along without telling me first? I thought it was weird that she said she'd stay at a hotel this time. For a while, I was afraid that maybe you guys didn't get along last time or something. She told you about him when she was here, right?"

His memory of their time together was taking a beating, along with his pride. He didn't really want to hear more, but Aaron didn't even have to respond and Emery forged ahead.

"Of course she did, she's always going on and on about him. Fucker. They're really tight. Well, we are too, we have the baseball thing. But he's more like her, kinda serious and studious. Into art and history and all that shit. He's always dragging her out to galleries and museums."

Aaron felt ill, and he was definitely done listening. He hadn't even known she was into that kind of stuff, but then again, they hadn't done much talking. He walked away, but found himself zeroing in on her in the stands, and sure enough, the tall, dark-haired man next to her had his arm possessively around her shoulders. As Emery had called him — *fucker.*

The game was a close one, and Aaron was thankful for the distraction. Emery played a fantastic game, going three for four at the plate and having a spotless defensive game at third. Every time Aaron looked up into the stands, Teri and the guy were hanging all over each other, so he'd finally stopped looking.

What the hell was he doing anyway? He should've headed back to the team weeks ago.

Yeah, you were just hanging around waiting for Teri to show back up.

Well, that's obviously not going to happen anymore.

Time to get back home and get back to work. Rehab was going fine here, but he needed the atmosphere of his own team to motivate him. He approached Coach. "Hey, you got a sec?"

* * * *

Teri watched as Aaron gave her — she thought — yet another cold look. Maybe it was just conceit that made her think she was the object of his interest among the thousands of people in the stands. Or maybe wishful thinking. She sighed.

Oh, come on, her inner critic scolded. *He made it very clear that he had lost interest in you when he told you not to bother to come to his room that night. Must've been the memory of the very clear view of your old lady body in the shower.*

That brutal experience didn't help her get over her crazy hot, immediate and lasting attachment to him. Time and distance hadn't done the trick either. The past month had been the longest she'd ever gone without seeing Emery in his entire life. She'd justified it to herself and to him by telling him the partial truth, that he needed to learn to do things for himself and stand on his own two feet without her to bail him out. He had really come around and had earned a spot on the roster of the club's AAA team, only one step below the Majors.

Without the need to avoid Aaron, Teri didn't know if she would have thought to separate herself from Emery like that, so she had him to thank for helping to straighten Emery out, in more ways than one. Her need to see Emery had finally beaten out her pride, and she'd planned this trip, hoping to get the chance to get Aaron out of her system somehow.

Teri sighed again, and Alex rolled his eyes. "You sound like you've sprung a leak."

She shot an irritated glance up at him.

"Seriously, Ma. Just chill. You'll get a chance to be with him soon. I know you've really missed him. It hard to be apart from someone you love."

For a minute, she froze, her brain translating that to mean Aaron. Because she *had* really missed him.

But do I love him? Could I have fallen that fast?

"Mom?" Alex gave her a concerned look. "You okay?"

"I'm okay, Alex, just thinking."

I have to see him, then I'll know.

As soon as the game was over, she was on the phone to Emery. "Hey, hon, why don't you ask Aaron to come along to dinner with us?"

"I already tried. He said he just wants to go home."

She thought fast. "I'm sure that Alex wants to see where you're living." Alex gave her a startled look. "We'll meet you over there instead of at the restaurant. But, uh, don't tell Aaron we're coming. I want to surprise him."

Alex's enquiring look had turned penetrating and suspicious and, judging from the silence on the other end of the line, she would bet a million bucks Emery had an identical expression on his face. Really, it would've been one of those comical 'twin moments', but for the adrenaline racing through her system at the thought of seeing Aaron face-to-face again.

"Sure, Ma. Sounds good. See you there." Emery's voice was unnatural, so Aaron must've been standing right there. Her heart beat fast as she said goodbye.

As soon as she hung up, she held a hand up. "Don't even start, Alex."

"Uh-huh."

Chapter Fourteen

Teri felt like she was about to jump out of her skin as they finally pulled into the condo complex to find both Emery's and Aaron's vehicles there ahead of them. Alex was driving, silent except for glances that spoke volumes. He pulled in near Em's truck and parked, turned resolutely toward her, with an expression she knew brooked no argument.

"Okay, Ma. I get that you don't want to talk about this, but there's no way I'm walking in there completely blind. Give me something to go on here."

Teri took a deep breath. Might as well just tell the truth. "I think I might've fallen for Em's roommate."

With that, she got out of the car and, before she could change her mind, headed toward Aaron's building. She heard the murmur of Alex's voice behind her and she stopped at the bottom of the stairs, turning in time to see him putting his phone in his pocket. It only took Alex's long legs a few more moments to catch up with her, but he simply gave her a hard side-hug and walked up the stairs with her to the door, trailing her inside when Emery let them in.

"Hey." Her normally chatty son was seemingly at a loss for words, eyeing her in disbelief. Alex had definitely given him the low-down on her bombshell.

She gave him a hug. "Great game, Emery. I'm so impressed. You've really been working hard, haven't you?"

Emery shrugged and walked over to greet Alex.

"Hey, bro, nice game." Alex ruffled Emery's hair. "Jeez, it's going to be as long as Ma's soon."

"Fuck off." Emery finally smiled, gave in to a rough hug then turned with Alex as they heard a voice behind them.

"Did I hear a knock…?" Aaron trailed off and came to a dead stop at the sight of three of them.

Teri's pulse spiked as she drank in the sight of him, just out of the shower with his hair finger-combed and few stray droplets of water still trickling down his neck. He looked delicious, and memories of their shower, their other times together and the promise of more, flooded through her.

Aaron's expression flashed from anger to confusion as his eyes flicked back and forth between the boys and Teri. "This is Alex? Alex is your son?" He sounded surprised, but there was a deeper emotion there she couldn't put her finger on.

"Yeah, he's my other half, literally," Emery joked.

Alex elbowed him. "You mean your better half."

Em shoved back. "Ha, just because you shoved your way out first—"

A brief scuffle for supremacy broke out, the boys' traditional way of saying hello, but Teri and Aaron only had eyes for one another.

"Uh, we're going out."

"Don't wait up."

The words barely penetrated, but the slamming of the door brought Teri to her senses at last. Realizing the boys had gone, she finally found her voice.

"Hi, Aaron."

"Hi."

She searched his face for something, anything to give her a hint as to what he was thinking. *C'mon, girl, just put it out there.* "I missed you."

"I missed you too." He took three big strides, then she was in his arms, their lips coming together with a month's worth of deprivation. She poured everything she was into making love to his mouth, showing him without words how she had dreamt of and hoped for this very thing.

She couldn't get close enough and gave a frustrated hop. Aaron caught her ass in his hands as she wrapped her legs around him. Oh, shit.

She attempted to pull away, and he followed with his lips, swallowing part of her words. "Stop, your shoulder—"

"'S'fine, been rehabbing. Kiss me back."

Teri moaned into his mouth as she obeyed and felt her world tilt around her as he whirled around and strode down the hall to his room, kicking the door closed behind them then deliberately lowering her to the bed and covering her with his welcome weight.

"Yes, yes," she mumbled encouragement, as he slid his lips along her cheek to the hollow of her jaw.

His voice reflected his need, gruff and hoarse. "We need to talk."

"Talk later, this now."

"No." He reluctantly pulled away to half-recline next to her, reaching behind his neck to gently remove her hands. "You have to know something before this happens. *If* it's going to happen."

It was like a dash of cold water, the way he sounded as if he was confessing something. She stopped fighting to hold him and gave him her full attention, patting his chest with her hand. "Okay, Aaron. What is it?" She was proud of how reasonable her voice sounded, considering all the emotions whirling about inside her.

His green eyes pinned hers. "I'm going back to my team this week."

Teri was torn. On the one hand, he was moving away, but on the other…

"That's great news. Your shoulder must be doing better."

He stared at her. "It is. Teri"—he frowned as he clarified—"you know that means I'll be leaving here. Within the next couple days."

Her heart swelled at his uncertain look. She continued to stroke his pecs, tracing the swells of muscle before gently smoothing over his troublesome shoulder.

"I know. And apparently you've forgotten I don't have a problem traveling." She arched her brow. "Especially when it comes to baseball."

"Mmm." Aaron tackled her and rolled them over so she was astride him. "You did that thing with your eyebrow again. Why does that turn me on?"

"Oh, only my eyebrow turns you on?" Teri rolled her hips against his, delighted by the hard ridge she rode.

"*Even* your eyebrow turns me on. Every part of you does." He pulled her down into a hug, nuzzling her neck. "You are the sexiest, most loving woman I've ever known. I'm so glad you're—" Aaron stopped and froze.

Teri rose up just a bit to meet his gaze. "I'm yours. If you want me," she finished for him, deciding to go for broke. "I can't believe I fell in love with you in two days."

Her world tilted again as he reversed their positions with stunning speed. "Tell me again," he demanded.

She couldn't dream of playing coy. "I love you, Aaron."

"Oh, God, Ter, I love you too. I was going crazy trying to figure out what went wrong and I couldn't stop thinking about you. It's been a hellish month. Don't you ever keep us apart that long again," he added fiercely.

"Hey," she began to protest. It wasn't just her fault.

But he went on with barely a pause, "And I won't do anything stupid like imply I don't want you in my bed. God, I was an idiot that night. What was I thinking?" he bemoaned. "We could've has this"—he thrust against her—"for the past month. Damn it."

"Let's not waste any more time. Strip." She gave him a push and they both got naked in record time, Aaron landing atop her again. God! The feeling of his warm, bare skin anchoring her to the mattress was heavenly. Then they were kissing again, rocking together, needing to connect on the most basic level, to sate their need, but also to reassure and build a foundation.

He nibbled and licked his way down her body, concentrating for a long while on her breasts, which seemed to have a direct connection to her clit, every tug and suck translating itself into a growing need for him to get down there, damn it, and soon. As if reading her mind, he slid lower and slowly, deliberately parted her folds, running his tongue through her wetness then upwards. Teri watched as he spread her own moisture with his tongue, laving her clit along each side repeatedly then taking it in a hard suck, which had her throwing her head back helplessly. He punctuated the suction with a flick of his tongue, then the next draw had her coming. With his hands gripping her hips, she surrendered to the waves crashing over her.

"I have to get inside you." Aaron groaned, then crawled up to cradle her head in his hands. "Do we have to worry about birth control? I'm clean—I haven't been with anyone since before my injury last fall. But I have condoms if you want to wait for proof."

Teri touched his face as warmth spread through her, loving his serious concern, but had no intention of having anything between them this first time.

"I trust you. It's been years for me—I'm good too, and I get the shot. C'mon." She reached between them and took his silky, steel-hard erection in her hand, savoring the heft of him and the slippery glide of pre-cum easing her thumb's exploration of the head.

He adjusted his position and she rubbed the tip of his cock against her own slick entrance. Removing her hand, she left the moment of entry up to him, and kissed him for all she was worth, humming as he slowly pushed his way into her.

This was what she'd been dreaming about and anticipating for the past month, and their eyes communed silently as he held himself over her, each slow thrust rubbing his pubic hair over her sensitive clit as his girth stretched her repeatedly on each entry. His pace quickened and she held on for the ride, her gaze never leaving his face as the tautness there gave way to a look of repletion. He raised himself up as he pressed and held tight within her, jerking a bit in his aftermath before collapsing over her and wrapping her in a tight embrace.

Her heart soared as they floated back to earth, fitting together as if they'd been custom made for one another. Teri smiled against his neck, running her hands over his smooth back, unable to stop touching him now that she had the right.

"What's the smile for?" He braced himself up on his forearms on either side of her head.

"Just happy." And that was the whole truth and nothing but. Everything she was feeling right now could be boiled down to sheer and utter happiness.

"We gonna make this work?" he asked, but it felt more like a statement.

"Mm-hmm. Spring training's over. Time we made a team."

"A team of two," he paused. "Well, four. Are they going to be okay with us?"

Teri grinned. "Why do you think they took off and said not to wait up? So, Mr Reynolds, you're going to sign on with us?"

"A permanent, lifetime contract, if you'll have me."

"Oh, I'll have you." Teri pulled him down. "Play ball."

About the Author

After living all over the US while growing up, I've settled into the beautiful Pacific Northwest and can't see myself living anywhere else. I'm a mom to two girls, who—to my pride and gratification—love to read and want to make a living with words themselves someday.

Even when I'm not writing, I find myself storing up experiences and people for future reference. I had decades of potential material at my mental fingertips by the time I started putting my stories into words.

I believe that passion is to be treasured, stepping out of the box should be encouraged, and forever can come from the most unlikely of beginnings. So find a story, step inside and immerse yourself in the magic of love. I'll meet you there…

Stacey Lynn Rhodes loves to hear from readers. You can find her contact information, website details and author profile page at http://www.totallybound.com.

Totally Bound Publishing

www.ingramcontent.com/pod-product-compliance
Lightning Source LLC
Chambersburg PA
CBHW030139180626
46812CB00002B/755

* 9 7 8 1 7 8 4 3 0 0 8 1 4 *